EMBER

Ember Book 1

EMMA SLATE

Prologue

MONSTERS DON'T LIVE in the dark.

They don't lurk under beds or hide in closets.

They don't have fangs or claws or fur.

Monsters wear facades.

They hide behind white smiles and forced geniality.

They walk around in broad daylight, wearing five-thousand-dollar, custom-made suits and expensive loafers.

Monsters make golden promises.

They dry your tears with their initialed handkerchiefs, all the while planning your demise.

They want every part of you and then some.

Monsters don't live in the dark.

They *are* the dark.

Chapter One

DRUNKEN IRISHMEN WERE the absolute worst. They were ribald and boisterous, they were nostalgic for a time they'd never lived, and they drank Jameson like it was their God-given right.

My father never touched Jameson. Called it undrink-able swill. His drink of choice was Bushmills.

Had been Bushmills.

I turned away from the cluster of men who were singing Irish drinking songs at the top of their lungs. The bar was bought out for the night, so there was no concern for bothering other patrons.

"Is it me? Or are they all off-key?" Shannon raised a blonde eyebrow and glanced at me with knowing blue eyes.

"Off-key. And it's just going to get worse." I grimaced and took a sip of Irish whiskey. I brushed my long dark hair off my shoulder as I looked back to her.

"It's your fault," she reminded me. "You're the one who sprang for an open bar."

I sighed. "You can't have an Irish wake without access to alcohol. It goes against the laws of nature. Besides, it's what Dad would've wanted." I pressed a finger to my temple. "If only Sean were here…"

"Still no idea where he is?"

"For all I know, he left the ashram and went to the Himalayas to gather pink salt. Who gets lost on a quest to find himself?"

"*Not all who wander are lost,*" Shannon quoted.

Sean had been wandering for the past five years, only popping up in Boston randomly. He never stayed long. Even across the world, I thought my older brother would still have kept tabs on Dad's condition, so then he could come home, pay his respects.

No respects had been given, and Sean hadn't called in weeks.

I grabbed the bottle of Bushmills resting on the bar and refilled my glass. I pointed it at her, but she shook her head. "Thanks. But I'm the one who's driving."

"Right." I sighed and set the bottle aside, turning my back to the group of Irishmen.

The first few hours of my father's wake had been almost unbearable. So many well-wishers, members of the Boston community, and business colleagues had paid their respects and wanted to talk about Michael O'Malley, esteemed real estate developer. I'd smiled and nodded, not listening to any of it. At least they were gone now and those left at The Speckled Hen were friends and those my father had considered family. Drunken friends and family.

"Do you want me to go with you tomorrow?" Shannon asked. "Sean's not here, and Jessica…"

Jessica, my father's young widow, had been no help the last week. She'd taken to her bed like a dramatic Victorian heroine. She'd come to the wake, popping in for an hour and then vanishing. She was headed to a grief spa, whatever the hell that was.

I'd been the one to rally. I'd been the one to see to my father's last wishes. I'd been the one to organize the service and the wake. And tomorrow, I'd be the one to sit across from my father's lawyer and listen to the reading of the will.

"No," I said, my voice surprisingly strong. "No, I'll go alone. Thanks, Shannon."

"You sure? Because it's really no—"

"I'm sure."

Her hand gripped her glass of water, but she didn't move to take a drink. "A few years ago, you would've begged me to go with you."

My jaw hardened. "A few years ago, I was someone else entirely."

Her finger traced a wood grain of the scarred oak bar. "Have you heard—"

"No."

"Do you want—"

"And I don't want to talk about it, Shannon. Not now. Not ever."

She swallowed. "Okay." Her voice came out shaky, weak.

I softened immediately. "I'm sorry."

"No, it's my fault. I should have—"

"It's fine."

"It's not fine. You're not *fine*."

"Of course I'm not fine," I snapped. "I'm at my father's wake and you want to discuss *him*—You bring up—"

"You've been through a lot these last two years, Quinn. Not just with your dad, but with Sasha." She shook her head. "When you came back to Boston a year ago, I didn't push you into talking about him, hoping you'd confide in me. But you rarely mention him and it's like you've shoved it all down. I'm scared you're gonna blow."

"You have crap timing," I pointed out.

"There's no good time to talk about it. I'm worried about you. Patrick and I are worried about you."

"Will you drop it?" I stared hard at her. "Please? I can't do this now."

She paused a moment. "When *can* you do this?"

I pretended to think about it as I swallowed a heavy dose of whiskey. "Never. I can never do this."

Shannon stood up from her seat at the bar. "I should go."

"Maybe that's for the best."

I thought she'd leave, find Patrick and escape. She surprised me when she pulled me into a strong hug. "You're not alone, Quinn," she said into my shoulder.

Shannon was a good few inches shorter than me, so when she hugged me, I smelled the lavender of her conditioner. She pulled back but didn't let go of my arms. Her eyes searched mine. "Do you hear me?"

"I hear you."

"Do you believe me?"

It was easy to feel like you had people when you'd never lost anyone. Shannon hadn't suffered loss after loss. Both her parents were still alive. She was married to her high school sweetheart. She was happy and I was...

But I didn't want to fight or seem ungrateful. So I said, "Yeah, I believe you."

"Call if you need me," she said, finally releasing me.

"I will." I wouldn't.

With one last look at me, she went in search of her husband. I sat back down at the bar, glad to have a moment to myself. I wouldn't leave The Speckled Hen until the last Irishman succumbed to Jameson. Even if that meant staying until dawn. Or past dawn. It was what my father would've wanted. An O'Malley never left a party early.

"Quinn O'Malley," a deep voice said behind me. "Only you could look hot at a funeral."

I swiveled, a smirk appearing on my lips. "Adam McNeely. Only you could say something so inappropriate and get away with it."

"Well, when you look like this." He waved a hand down his tall, muscular form. His dark hair was flopping across his forehead, and his dark blue eyes twinkled in the dim light of the bar.

"You gonna hug me, or what?" he demanded.

A gurgle of laughter escaped as I threw myself into his strong arms. He smelled of Gucci and expensive hair products.

"Richard sends his regrets he couldn't be here. Hannah has the flu."

"Ugh."

"Yeah. Babies are cute until they throw up all over you. She's mine, and I love her, but God. Something is always coming out of her!"

I laughed and he smiled. That had been Adam's intent all along. He'd always been good at that. He hadn't been labeled "class clown" our junior year for nothing.

"How is *Quinn*?"

"Quinn is fine."

"Quinn is lying." Adam looked at the bartender and gestured for a glass. "And Quinn seems entirely too sober for this occasion."

"How does Adam know that Quinn is lying?" I demanded, pouring him a shot of Bushmills.

"Because Adam is one of Quinn's oldest friends, and

he can read her like a book. Also, Quinn and Adam are at Quinn's father's wake."

"Do you think Adam and Quinn can stop talking about themselves in the third person?"

"Sure. Though, I think I kind of like it." He raised his glass to me. I lifted mine, and we clinked.

"*Sláinte*," we both said at the same time before downing our whiskey.

"Shit, that's good. I forgot how good." He wiped his mouth with a bar napkin and then took a seat next to me. "Why are you alone? Where is Shannon? And Patrick?"

"Shannon just left. Patrick was drunk before the sun set."

"Why aren't you drunk?"

"Someone has to hold it all together."

"Ah."

We fell silent as I repoured our drinks. Maybe the idea of getting completely hammered wasn't such a bad idea. I wasn't driving—and complete annihilation might mean I could actually sleep tonight.

That was the hope, anyway.

"Jessica isn't here?" he asked, looking around for my stepmother. The woman was only five years older than me. Memories from the family dinner three years ago when I'd first met her had me grimacing.

"She was here earlier for a minute and a half. She left." I shrugged. I didn't care that much that she wasn't here. It wouldn't have made me feel any better. Still, I was the only representative for the O'Malley family. A lone reed.

"The will?" Adam asked.

"Tomorrow."

I shot back more whiskey, loving the burn, missing it. I'd been on a vodka kick for a while, but vodka just wouldn't do at an Irish wake.

Maybe a Russian wake.

Did Russians have wakes?

I'd have to ask—

"Quinn?"

"Hmm?" I looked at Adam.

"You want to come stay with us?"

I smiled. "Shannon offered me the same thing."

"For you to come stay with Richard and me?"

"No." Shaking my head, I set the glass aside. I could already feel the nostalgia swimming to the surface. Though a wake was the place for nostalgia, mine would be more than melancholic. And that was something I didn't want to dive into.

"You sure?"

"Yeah." I sighed. "I'm thinking about doing some traveling."

"Oh?"

"Yeah. This last year...it was hard...even before Dad. I think I just need to get out of Boston for a while."

Adam knew better than to ask. Shannon had always been the one to push me into talking about things. Adam never pushed.

I used to talk. A lot. About everything and nothing.

"Where are you thinking of going?" Adam swirled his glass of Bushmills and then took a sip, blue eyes on me.

"Ireland."

"Ah."

"I've got family friends there," I pointed out. Family friends who hadn't been able to step foot in the United States, considering they were on the most wanted list.

"Then maybe you should go somewhere else. Like Italy. I hear they have great wine tours."

"I've heard that, too." My eyes went back to my glass,

and I was debating another shot, but I looked away when I heard Adam's sharp inhale.

"Dear God All Mighty, the hottest guy I've ever seen just walked in. Forget traveling—have a hot one-night stand with this guy."

Curious, I rotated my head. My eyes narrowed.

Dark blue eyes, the color of cobalt, found mine. His angular jaw clenched as he approached.

"Holy shit, he's coming over here!" Adam breathed.

The man stopped in front of my bar chair. He loomed over me, and I was a tall woman, even when seated.

"Hello, Quinn." His Scottish brogue was thick and layered with remorse.

Anger and bitterness coated my tongue. "Hello, Flynn."

Chapter Two

"You know him?" Adam stage-whispered.

I didn't take my eyes off Flynn Campbell, the Scottish hotel mogul whom I'd once called friend. "Yes. I know him."

When it was clear I wasn't going to introduce Flynn to Adam, Flynn's eyes slid away. He brought his right hand out from his long gray wool coat

"Flynn Campbell."

"Adam McNeely. I'm an old friend of Quinn's from high school," he explained, shaking Flynn's hand. "How do you know Quinn?"

"I used to be friends with Flynn's wife," I stated flatly.

Adam frowned, dropping Flynn's hand.

"Will you excuse us?" the Scotsman asked Adam.

"Sure," Adam said easily. I knew his curiosity was going haywire, but he managed to contain it. His eyes found mine, silently asking if I wanted to be left alone with Flynn. I nodded. Adam took his glass, poured me more Bushmills, and then left.

Left me with Flynn Fucking Campbell.

"What the hell are you doing here?" I asked, unable to hide the anger in my tone.

"I came to pay my respects."

"Okay. You paid them. You can leave now."

Flynn's gaze was unflinching. Unyielding. At one point in time, I thought I knew the man standing in front of me. I thought I knew a lot of things.

How wrong I'd been.

It only took one fire to burn everything to the ground. Literally.

"Will you be insulted if I drink Scotch?"

"Yes," I said without thought. "I'll also be insulted if you stay."

He sighed.

"I don't want you here," I said through gritted teeth.

He acted as though he hadn't heard me. The bartender was busy, so Flynn leaned over and filched a rocks glass from the clean stack and then poured himself a drink from the bottle of Bushmills. He grimaced after he took a sip.

"This is vile. How can you drink it?" He looked at me, dark eyebrow raised.

"Really? You flew all the way from Scotland to insult Irish whiskey?"

"No." He paused. "I flew all the way from Scotland to pay my respects to you. And to tell you that she misses you."

"Okay, so she misses me."

"Quinn—"

I stood up, clutching my glass of whiskey, wanting to hurl it but not wanting to be the center of attention. "No!" I took a deep, steadying breath. "No, Flynn. You don't get to do this. You don't get to come to my father's wake and tell me… You just *can't*."

"You're not the only one who has suffered. The last

two years have been difficult—for all of us," he lashed out, patience finally at an end. "Do you know what we went through? What my wife went through?"

"Yes," I snapped. "I know." I leaned in close, got in his face. "You act like you're the only two people that have lived through any sort of tragedy."

He took a step closer, his nose grazing mine. "That's not why you're mad. That's not why you've stopped taking Barrett's calls."

"She knows where he is," I gritted out.

"Aye."

"Do you?"

He took a breath, stepped back, looked away. "Aye."

"And neither one of you will tell me." Anger suddenly gave way to sadness. "You chose him. You chose to protect him, to keep his secrets."

"He wants you to be happy," Flynn said.

"I was happy."

"You weren't."

"I would've been. *We* would've been. If he had just given it some time. He was finally healing. We were finally healing."

"He gave it over a year," he pointed out.

"If it had been you," I said, "would you have left Barrett?"

He paused, obviously weighing his words. I knew I wasn't going to like whatever came out of his mouth.

"We have the bairns, Quinn. It's not the same."

I was right—I hadn't liked what Flynn said.

"He left me, Flynn. I came home one day and he was just...gone. A note on the counter..."

I'd burned the note in the fireplace, wanting no trace of it. Didn't matter, the words would never turn to ash.

I'm not the man I used to be, Myshka. He is dead. Mourn me and love again.

I'd destroyed everything in the kitchen. All the plates, the glasses. I'd taken a bottle of vodka, drank a third of it, and then threw the rest in the fireplace. After I sobered up, I'd left for Boston. I moved back home—and left my life with Sasha behind. Or tried to. But just because you changed cities didn't mean the memories of a living ghost didn't haunt you.

My father hadn't asked any questions when I walked through the door of my childhood home. He didn't need to.

"Quinn," Flynn began, bringing me back to the present, back to the bar where I was supposed to be celebrating the life of my father.

"Don't, Flynn. Don't make any excuses. They aren't yours to make."

He threw back the rest of his whiskey and set his glass down on the bar. "She misses you."

"No, she doesn't. She misses him."

"She does miss him," he agreed.

I cocked my head to the side. "That bothers you—that she misses him."

"Does it bother you?"

"It only bothers me if he's in communication with her."

"He's not."

The knob of tension inside of me released. "So, he's not talking to anyone, then."

"No one that I know of," Flynn admitted. "And you're wrong."

"About?"

"Barrett. She misses you. In your own right. Not by extension."

"It's not enough, Flynn."

"I know."

"Is he ever…" I couldn't bring myself to ask, not all the way.

"I don't know. I don't know if he's ever coming back. Do you really want him to? He's not the man you fell in love with."

"Yes, he is," I stated. "You don't stop loving people because they change." Sasha had changed. Not just physically. The accident had shaken something loose in his soul.

I grasped the bottle of Bushmills by the neck. The glass was cool in my hand. "What are you trying to do here?"

"I'm not sure," he admitted with a wry smile. "I thought—maybe I could talk you into—"

"Into what?"

"A visit. To Scotland. Don't you want some time away from Boston?"

I did, but I wouldn't give him the satisfaction of telling him that. "Why didn't Barrett come?" I demanded. "If she's so upset about our estrangement, why didn't she come and talk to me herself?"

"She was afraid you'd deck her." He smiled for a moment and then it slipped. "She is here, Quinn. In Boston."

"Barrett's here?"

"Aye."

I looked away from him.

"All right, Quinn." He sighed. "All right."

It was on the tip of my tongue to apologize, but I stopped myself. What was I apologizing for? My feelings? I was entitled to them.

I pitched my voice low despite the drunken, boisterous Irishmen who were yelling at the top of their lungs. "She hurt me."

"I know."

"You hurt me."

"I know."

I looked him in the eyes when I admitted, "But he destroyed me. I've got nothing left, Flynn. For anyone."

Chapter Three

THE LAST IRISHMAN succumbed to Jameson at 3:14 AM. I was sure of the exact time because I had my cell phone out, my thumb pressing the number to call my personal driver. I climbed into the back of the black town car and sank into the leather seat. Closing my eyes, I murmured something to Donovan, and then we were moving.

"How was it?" he asked, his Irish lilt still thick despite living in the States for thirty years.

The divider between the front and back seat was down. It was always down. Donovan had been one of my father's most trusted employees. He'd known me my entire life. I'd grown up calling him Uncle Donovan. It was odd to think that I'd inherited him and his servitude. I made a mental note to increase his salary. He wouldn't take it.

"You didn't stop in?" I asked.

Even in the early Boston morning, I saw his eyes meet mine in the rearview mirror. "I was there. For a moment."

I smiled softly. "Which corner were you sitting in?" My gaze slid away from his. Donovan had always looked out for me. Even when I hadn't been able to look out for myself.

"You drank a fair bit," he pointed out. "But you didn't get sloppy."

"I haven't been sloppy in years."

He chuckled. I wondered if he was remembering my years as a teenager. My hell-raising years. Everyone always worried about their sons turning into hellions. Sons had nothing on a motherless teenage girl who wanted her father's attention.

"You don't miss teaching me how to drink Bushmills like I was one of the boys?"

"Too pretty to be a boy, Quinn. I just wanted you to learn how to handle yourself in a man's world. Our world."

"You gave me some pretty good survival skills," I admitted.

"Would it do me any good to tell you I'm worried about you?"

"You wouldn't be the first." I scrunched my toes but refused to take off the heels. I wouldn't be able to get them back on. My feet had gone numb hours ago. Along with everything else. "Do you ever feel like…you're swimming, but everything around you is so far away, out of touch? You can't really see or hear. So you keep throwing your hands out, hoping to—I don't know—catch something. Like a rope. Anything that will pull you *out.*"

Donovan didn't say anything for a long time. So long that I thought we'd ride out the rest of the car trip in silence. But then he spoke. "How long have you been swimming, Quinn?"

Too long. Since Sasha. Since his accident. Which had changed both of us. "Two years, maybe? I don't know. I've lost track of time."

There was the year that Sasha was bedridden. Burned all the way to his soul. And just when I thought he was healing, he'd left. This past year had been hell. Grieving a broken heart, and then my father dying.

So many losses. Sasha, my father…

I couldn't think about the others.

"Do you think I should take a vacation?" I asked.

"No. Your life will still be here waiting for you when you get back. You'll get through this. *All* of this. O'Malleys don't run."

I snorted. I'd done exactly that. Sasha had left me and what did I do? I'd run home to my father's house.

The car pulled to a stop outside the home that was full of memories of deceased people.

I didn't want to move. I didn't want to go in there, which is why I reached for the door. Before I could get it open, Donovan was there and he helped me out of the car. Then he wrapped me in a tight hug.

"Phone is on," he said gruffly, pulling back.

I nodded and pressed a soft kiss to his clean-shaven cheek. I looked over my shoulder at the house I'd grown up in and forced myself to take a step toward it. And then another. I didn't look back at Donovan. If I did, I might beg him to stay there with me in that large, empty house just so I wouldn't feel so alone.

But I had to do it alone. Everything alone.

I unlocked the door and turned to give Donovan a wave. He got back into the car, and then I shut the front door. Without turning on the foyer light, I sank down to the floor, pulled my knees up to my chest, and tried to make myself as small as possible.

Eventually, I got up. I finally took off my heels, giving a small groan of relief as my swollen feet were allowed to breathe.

I locked up the house and strolled down the hallway—past the living room, past the sitting room, past the dining room, past all the empty rooms that no one had any use for, and into the kitchen. I didn't stop there. Opening the sliding glass doors, I was hit with a blast of cold Boston air. I shivered.

My feet chilled the moment they stepped onto the stone. The heated pool was uncovered, and I dipped my toes in just for a second before making my way to the newly remodeled pool house. Though small, it was actually comfortable. I breathed a sigh of relief when I got inside. It was warm and my fingers and toes thawed.

I went over to the liquor cart and grasped the bottle of vodka. Maybe it was a terrible idea to drink vodka after drinking whiskey all night long, but...

"Glass or no glass?" I asked no one. "No glass, it is. Why dirty crystal? Am I right?"

I took the bottle of vodka and plunked down on the couch. I rarely drank alone, but if there was any night to drink by yourself, it was the night of your father's wake.

Chapter Four

THE ALARM on my phone blared, jarring me awake. Morning rays peeked through the windows, causing me to squint. Somehow, I'd fallen asleep sitting up, clutching the bottle of vodka. I couldn't remember if I'd actually taken a drink or not. I set the bottle on the coffee table and stood.

My body protested. Between lack of sleep, a light supper, and a lot of alcohol, I felt like a piece of road kill.

But I didn't have time to feel that way. I had a meeting with my father's lawyer in two hours, and I needed to get it together. I picked up my phone and headed for the door. As I crossed the patio, I called Jessica.

She didn't answer her phone. Shocker. No doubt she was getting all the grief massaged out of her.

"Jessica," I said, my tone terse. "The will is being read today. Just thought I'd remind you. Again. Meeting is at eleven."

I hung up, a swift wave of anger knocking me in the chest.

My father had loved two women in his life. One of them had been my mother. The other... Jessica was nothing like my mother. My mother had been a partner. Jessica had been someone my father had to take care of.

I was someone my father had had to take care of.

I went back to the main house to shower and change. My uniform these days consisted of black dresses. Trendy black dresses, but black dresses nonetheless. So no one would have any doubt that Michael O'Malley's daughter was in mourning. After two cups of coffee and a dry piece of toast, I called Donovan.

The morning was gray and cold. I shrugged into a long black coat, wrapped a charcoal-colored cashmere scarf around my neck, and waited for Donovan on the porch. I was down the steps the moment Donovan pulled into the driveway.

"You could've waited inside," he said, holding open the passenger door for me.

I said nothing as I slid inside the warm car. The heat was on and my icy ears began to thaw.

"You look nice," Donovan commented.

"Hmmm."

Donovan fell silent, realizing I wasn't in the mood for conversation.

The law office was in the heart of bustling downtown. Checking in with the receptionist, I glanced around the quiet elegance of the waiting room. I sat down in a brown leather chair and picked up an architecture magazine and flipped through it, not seeing the pictures, not even bothering to read the captions.

"Ms. O'Malley?"

I looked up and stood.

The middle-aged man strode toward me, hand outstretched. He wore a crisp white shirt, a thick power tie, and a black suit. "Dave Flannigan.

"Call me Quinn," I said automatically.

"Quinn." He nodded. "I'm sorry we're meeting under these circumstances."

I wanted to tell him not to bother with the condolences, but I forced myself to smile graciously. "Thank you."

"Is there—Are we waiting for anyone else?"

"No. Just me."

Dave's face was blank, giving nothing away. He was probably good at his job. Held things close to the vest. Stepping aside, he gestured to the hallway. He led me to his office, a large corner room with high windows and a view of the gray city. Red Sox paraphernalia graced every wall. Autographed baseballs sat in front of tomes of law books. Photographs of him and the team through the years were tacked up on the walls.

He chuckled when he saw my gaze. "I have a bit of a problem. The Red Sox are my vice. The firm has seats behind home plate. Are you a baseball person?"

"No."

My abruptness didn't seem to faze him. He gestured for me to sit. I sat in the chair in front of his massive wood desk. There was one 8 X 5 ornate silver frame, angled just enough that I could see a woman, two children—a boy and a girl—and Dave. They were all smiling like goofs.

"My family," he said, picking up the photo and holding it out to me. I took it and stared at the happy, quintessential family. I expected to feel anger and resentment. Instead, I felt…happy. Smiling slightly, I handed it back to him.

"They're lovely."

"Thank you." He set the photo aside, took a moment to angle it just so, and then gave me his undivided attention. "Ms. O'Malley—Quinn. I knew your father a long time. Once, we were just two friends, struggling through classes at BC, and then one day, he was at the forefront of the real estate market, and he was asking me to be his lawyer." His brown eyes softened.

"You weren't at the wake," I said. "You weren't in the line of well-wishers."

He smiled in somber humor. "He asked me not to go. He said you would've hated to hear empty platitudes."

Tears formed behind my eyes, but I shoved them back. "My father knew me well."

"His will is a bit…unusual. But then again, so was he. He left Mrs. O'Malley a generous sum and the house. Enough that she will be well taken care of for the remainder of her life. To your brother, he left a sum as well." He paused. "To you, he left the rest."

Shaking my head, I frowned. "I'm afraid I don't understand."

"The business, Quinn. You've inherited your father's business."

Chapter Five

"I *WHAT?*"

"Inherited your father's—"

"Yes. I heard you. But, why?" I demanded. "I don't know anything about real estate developing."

"Apparently your father thought otherwise."

My father's business, his legacy, was now in the hands of his daughter. A daughter who had once been a teen model and who'd had no desire to do anything aside from shop and get her nails done. A daughter who had once been frivolous and selfish and had driven away the only man she'd ever loved.

"Mr. Flannigan, you know what I got a degree in? Communications. You do know what that means, right?"

"I—"

"It means I was expected to marry well, stand by my husband's side, throw parties, host events. Not *this*. Not run a hundred-million-dollar company into the ground."

"Your father wanted more for you, Quinn. More than you wanted for yourself."

I shook my head. "When?"

"Excuse me?"

"When was this will made?"

He hesitated.

It was enough. I knew. Dad had changed it when I'd left New York and come home to Boston. He wanted to give me something. When I had nothing.

The tears were behind my eyes, a mixture of grief and anger, of resentment and love, of obligation and honor.

"How? How can I do this?"

"My advice?" he asked with a soft smile. "Go into the office. Start there."

I rose, clutching my purse and coat close to my body, as if that were enough to keep all the feelings inside me. "Thank you for your time."

He stood and reached into his breast pocket of his suit jacket. "My card. Call me. Any time. Day or night. Your father had faith in you, Quinn. Maybe you should have a little faith in yourself."

"I had no idea lawyers were so naïve," I quipped, taking the card and clenching it in between my fingers.

He smiled. "Let me walk you out."

Thankfully, he didn't keep up any idle conversation as he saw me to the elevator. I stepped out of the building and into the cold. Instead of heading for the town car waiting for me, I just...walked.

In six-hundred-dollar heels.

I walked around the city, trying to understand what my father had seen in me, why he'd believed I had more potential than I ever gave myself credit for.

My father gave me half of Boston, and I'd never felt more alone.

"Quinn," Donovan shouted. The window of the driver's side was rolled down, his weathered face blustery with a frown. "Stop this. Get in."

"I don't want to," I said, feeling stubborn.

"It's been three hours. Come on. The temperature is dropping, and you're not wearing the appropriate clothing."

He had a point. I looked up at the gray sky, which was slowly turning white. Boston in winter was brutal. Especially if you weren't dressed for it. And I wasn't.

With a sigh, I stepped toward the car. Donovan hastily shifted into park, and then he was out, helping me with the door.

"Home?" he asked when we were both safe and warm in the heated car.

I shook my head. "Shannon's."

My best friend lived with her husband in a trendy downtown loft. Shannon had come from modest means and still believed in working. Patrick had not only come from old money, but he'd played for The Patriots. Blowing out his left knee had ended his career.

"Should I wait?" Donovan asked.

I shook my head. "I'll take a cab."

"I don't trust cabbies on icy roads."

Smiling at his concern, I shook my head. "I'll crash here for the night. I'll see you in the morning."

I got out of the car and hustled to the building. Snowflakes dusted my shoulders and eyelashes. Donovan had convinced me to get inside just in the nick of time.

Waving to the security guard who recognized me, I immediately went to the elevator. Patrick and Shannon lived in the penthouse. Shannon didn't really care where they lived, as long as she was allowed to decorate as she saw fit. Patrick loved her enough to let her, and he suffered through the white and cream décor.

I knocked on the door. A moment later, it opened. Shannon was dressed in a pair of old sweats, a pink thermal top, her blonde hair piled on top of her head in a messy bun. Her smile was wide and welcoming.

"Hi! What are you doing here?" she asked, embracing me before stepping back and letting me inside.

I picked up my leg to pull off my heel, groaning in relief.

"Here, let me get your coat," Shannon said before I could answer. "Oh. Is it snowing?"

"Just started," I explained. "Do you have any brandy?"

She frowned as she put my coat in the closet and shut the door. "Maybe. I don't know. Patrick might. I never drink the stuff."

Shannon was more of a red wine kind of girl.

"So, the will," she prodded as she headed for the kitchen. It was one of the best things about the loft. Large yet homey at the same time, despite the steel appliances, the white walls. There wasn't any clutter, yet the kitchen still looked warm and inviting. Shannon had that way about her.

"Brandy first," I said.

She nodded. "Got it. Let me see here." She began to open the cabinets where they kept the liquor. "Ah, thought so. Top shelf." Looking over her shoulder at me, she smiled. "Can you reach it? I can't. Not without a chair."

I plucked the bottle from the top shelf easily, laughing.

"What?" Shannon asked with a wry grin. "It's not my fault I'm short."

"I was just thinking about how I've been getting things off the tops of shelves since I was a sophomore in high school."

"That's what you get for sprouting early." Shannon took the bottle of brandy from my hands and went over to the corner of the living room where Patrick had a custom bar built. An old 1950s radio that still worked rested on the bar, a classy adornment. I ran my finger over the dials.

Shannon took out a snifter, held it up to the light, and deemed it clean. She poured me a small amount and then looked at me for confirmation.

"Ah, how about a little bit more."

She added a splash and then screwed on the bottle top.

"You're not going to have any?" I asked.

Shannon handed me the snifter. "No. Still a little bit early for me."

I took a small sip, letting the alcohol bloom on my taste buds before swallowing. Nothing like a good brandy to warm the insides, especially on a cold winter day.

"Come on." She gestured to the gray couch. "Let's sit and you can tell me everything."

Looking down into the amber liquid, I licked my lips, removing the traces of brandy. "My father gave me his business."

"His business?"

"Yup, in its entirety."

"What about Sean?"

"Monetary inheritance."

"And Jessica?"

I finally glanced at Shannon. Her blonde brows had nearly disappeared into her hairline. "Also a settlement."

"Your father gave you his entire business," Shannon said slowly. "Wow."

Downing the rest of the brandy, I closed my eyes, wanting to wash away the morning. "Yep. And I have no fucking idea what to do."

Chapter Six

Keys in the front door had me turning my head. Patrick appeared, holding grocery bags in one hand. He pulled off his gray wool beanie and tossed it, along with keys, onto the dark wood foyer table. He looked into the bags and didn't yet notice I was there.

"Babe, I got most of what you wanted, but they didn't have—"

"Quinn's here," Shannon said quickly.

Patrick's gaze lifted from the bags and a quick smile appeared on his lips. "Quinn. Hey."

I smiled. "Sorry to just show up."

"No worries." He went into the kitchen and set the bags on the counter before coming over to me.

I stood and gave him a hug before sitting back down. "You don't seem any worse for wear," I noted.

Patrick snorted. "I had to pop three Advil this morning." His face sobered as he placed a hand on Shannon's shoulder. "You went to the lawyer's this morning, didn't you?"

"Yeah." I sighed. "It seems I've inherited my father's company."

"No kidding." His eyes widened. "That's like a—"

"Multi-million-dollar company. I know." Leaning back against the sofa cushions, I desperately wanted to prop my feet up on the coffee table and take a load off, but I held it in. Even in Shannon's home, I kept it together. But if you couldn't fall apart in front of your best friend whom you'd known since you were five, who else could you fall apart in front of?

"I—well. I'm not sure what to say," Patrick admitted. He let go of Shannon's hand and moved toward the kitchen.

"Not much to say, I guess. I'm still in shock."

"Don't blame you for that. Ah, you've been in the brandy, I see," he teased, blue eyes flashing with humor.

I laughed. "Yeah. I couldn't convince your wife to have a glass with me."

"It's really early," she protested. "And I hate brandy."

Something about Shannon's tone had me pausing. I studied her. She wouldn't meet my gaze and dragged her nail across the cushion of the couch.

"You didn't drink last night, either," I remarked slowly.

"Someone had to be sober to drive," she reminded me.

"Yes. That's what you said at the wake." Cocking my head to the side, I drilled into her with my steady gaze. "But it was my father's wake. Surely Patrick could've stayed sober and let you drink yourself into oblivion with me."

Shannon bit a plump, pink lip and looked at Patrick for help.

Shooting up from the couch, I pointed at her. "You're pregnant!"

"I'm—well, yeah. Pregnant." Her eyes were beseeching and full of concern.

My mouth trembled. "You're pregnant," I repeated, quieter this time.

She nodded. "Quinn, I—"

Before she could get another word out, I leaned over and pulled her small, delicate frame against mine. "Oh, Shannon."

"You're not mad?" she whispered in my ear.

"Mad?" Rearing back, I stared her in the eyes. "Why would I be mad? You're having a baby. This is—This is exactly—Oh. Yay!"

Soft tears began to fall on her lashes and she smiled. "Really?"

Squeezing her hand, I looked at Patrick who was staring at his wife with a tender gaze that was intimate and private. Something passed between them. I watched it. And though my heart constricted when I recognized that look, a lovers' gaze, I pushed away any sadness.

"I'm going to be an auntie?" I asked with a huge grin.

"You're going to be an auntie," Shannon confirmed.

"Patrick," I said.

"Yeah, Quinn?"

"Have a brandy with me? We need to celebrate. And your wife is knocked up, so she can't drink with us."

"Sorry," he said with a roguish grin. "That's my fault."

We all laughed. Patrick fixed Shannon a glass of juice and then brought it to her. He went to the bar and grabbed a snifter. He took a seat next to his wife as I poured us some hefty drinks. I raised my glass.

"To new beginnings."

"To new beginnings," they echoed.

We all took sips of our drinks. The brandy burned its way down, but this time, it was accompanied by a surge of happiness instead of dread. I felt full when moments ago, I'd felt empty.

"So," I said, crossing my feet at the ankles. "Have you thought of a name?"

"Slow down," Shannon said, holding onto her glass. "I'm only eight weeks along."

"Yes. But you should be thinking about names now. And I have just the one for you."

"Oh?" Patrick asked in amusement, his arm wrapping around Shannon's shoulders and tugging her into his side.

"Quinn," I announced. "It's good for a boy or a girl."

Shannon chuckled. "Which is the argument your mother used on your father, right?"

"Exactly." I smiled in fond remembrance of my parents. "The woman always got what she wanted."

"Your father spoiled her rotten," Shannon said.

"He spoiled all his girls rotten," I said quietly. I raised the glass of brandy. "To Michael O'Malley."

"To Michael O'Malley," they echoed.

"To Michael O'Malley. What the fuck were you thinking, Dad?" I looked up at the ceiling, as if that would somehow make his form appear, and he could tell me why he'd given me his business.

"He always knew what he was doing," Patrick said. "Smartest man I knew."

Shannon raised her glass of juice. "To Quinn O'Malley. Who won't cock it up."

I sighed. "Who won't cock it up. Yeah, right."

Chapter Seven

I FELL asleep on the couch as the sun went down. Lulled by the warmth and by the comfort of being with close friends, it was easy to let my eyelids droop, the quiet sounds of Patrick and Shannon's conversation a soft security in the background.

I was used to falling asleep to white noise. I'd lived on the top floor of a warehouse loft in the Meatpacking District in Manhattan and was no stranger to the sounds of the city. I could fall asleep anytime, anywhere.

"I'm worried, Patrick," I heard Shannon say as I slowly resurfaced from sleep.

"I know. I am too."

"She hasn't been the same since he… And she won't talk about it."

"Stop trying to get her to talk about it," Patrick suggested.

"It's eating away at her. Have you seen how much weight she's lost?"

"Quinn has been through a lot this last year, Shannon. Let her grieve in her own way. In her own time."

"But she's not grieving," Shannon protested. "She's burying it. Her brother is God knows where. Sasha left. Her father died. She's alone."

"She's not alone. She has us."

"Not the same." Her voice had dropped to a murmur. "All the men in her life…"

Patrick paused. "What do you suggest we do? Tie her to a chair and make her talk?"

"If I thought I actually had your support to do that, then yeah," she admitted. "I just wish she'd open up. I'm her best friend. We used to talk about everything."

"This is different. But Quinn is stronger than she looks. You know that."

"Still…this has been a lot in such a short time." She hesitated. "What kind of man—Never mind."

"Go on," Patrick urged. "Get it off your chest."

"What kind of man lets a woman care for him while he heals, and the moment he's on his own two feet again, leaves her. He *left* her, Patrick. Left her in tiny broken pieces that she has no idea how to put back together."

"You really think Quinn is broken?"

"God, Patrick, have you seen her? The drinking? The wanting to be alone all the time, the not wanting to talk—"

"Not everyone wants to talk. And coping is coping. She gets up every day. Sometimes that's all you can expect."

My eyes opened, but I didn't say anything right away. I wasn't ready for them to realize that I'd heard their entire conversation.

Shannon's gaze left her husband's face and slid to mine. She swallowed. "How much of that did you hear?"

I sat up and stretched my neck to the side. "Enough."

"Are you mad?"

"No," I said, finding it to be true. "I just"—I ran my tongue across my teeth—"don't really know what I'm supposed to do. Talk about it? I don't even want to think about it, let alone talk about it." Talking about it just pissed me off and then made me sad.

Patrick and Shannon remained silent.

I stood. "I'm going to go."

"You don't have to," Patrick protested. "You can stay here tonight. The guest room has a new queen-sized bed."

"Thanks," I said, "but I think I want my own space. I want… Tomorrow is going to be…and I want to think about things."

Shannon rose and then walked over to embrace me. "Take care."

I smiled down at her. "You too."

"I'll drive you home. The snow's really coming down," Patrick volunteered.

Shaking my head, I embraced Patrick. "That's okay. Donovan will come get me." I grabbed my coat and put it on. "I'll call him from the lobby."

"Dinner?" Shannon piped up. "Sometime this week?"

"That would be nice."

With a wave, I left their apartment and let out a sigh of relief. I couldn't take their watchful gazes as they wondered when I was going to fall apart. I hadn't fallen apart when Sasha left. I hadn't fallen apart when my dad died.

I was Quinn O'Malley, and I didn't do falling apart.

People left, family died, and still the world turned. The world turned when all you wanted was it to stop, for just one moment, to grieve with you.

And if I ever saw Sasha Petrovich again, I'd punch him in the jaw just like my brother taught me. It would only be an ounce of what he deserved. Then again, I didn't really expect to see him again.

The last two years of my life had been brutal. I was

ready for something different. I was ready to throw myself into something new.

I guess it was fortuitous my father left me his company. I'd throw myself into that—I'd learn and absorb anything and everything I could. I didn't need people; I didn't need a partner. Work would be my lover. And it would it be constant and enough. I'd make it enough.

The elevator doors opened, and I stepped out into the lobby. I took a seat on one of the wooden benches and pulled my phone out of my purse to request an Uber. There was one ten minutes away.

"It's really coming down out there."

I glanced up and looked at the doorman, and then I peered out the lobby windows. Street lamps illuminated the heavy snowflakes. They fell in the path of the light before hitting the dusted sidewalk. The snow would stick tonight.

"Yeah, it looks like it's going to be a bad one," I said, not really in the mood for conversation.

"It's the kind of night where if you didn't have to be out, you wouldn't be," the doorman went on.

I nodded and realized he just wanted someone to talk at; he wasn't really expecting an answer. The Uber drove up and idled in front. I shot up from my seat, made sure I had everything, and headed for the door.

"Get home safe!" he called.

"You too!" I shot back.

A blast of cold air hit me in the face as I scrambled my way across the snowy sidewalk. I managed to get inside the warm car, but not before a good amount of flakes found their way into my heels.

Thankfully, the driver was quiet and not in the mood to talk. His focus was entirely on the drive. Ice already gripped the streets. There were sure to be many accidents that night. No better place for me to be than home, in front of a fire.

Alone.

All alone.

Twenty minutes later, I was climbing the porch steps to the house. My heel slipped on a patch of frost, and my ankle turned. My hands went out in front of me, but I still fell down, knees and palms hitting the stone steps.

I let out a stream of curses and closed my eyes as tears leaked out from the corners. Slowly, I got up. My right ankle throbbed, and I gingerly made my way into the house. I threw my coat and purse in the corner and flipped on the light.

The house was chilly; still in my heels, I hobbled over to the thermostat and turned it up a few degrees. I entered the den and turned on the gas fireplace. Grabbing the gray Irish wool blanket resting on the back of the couch, I favored my injured ankle. I took the blanket with me to the chair by the fire. I kicked off my left heel and then lifted my right ankle to rest on my knee. I gently worked off the pump and tossed it aside. My hose were torn at the knees, which were scraped, but aside from the ankle, I was fine. I should've propped it up and gotten some ice for it, but I didn't want to move.

Staring into the fireplace, I watched the flames dance. I got lost in the warmth and the flickering orange and yellow lulled me into a sleepy trance. When my ankle stopped hurting, I finally got up and climbed the staircase to the second floor. I didn't want to stay in the pool house tonight, nor did I want to sleep in my childhood room which was all white lace and frills. It was a reminder of the pampered life I'd had as a child.

After my mother died, my father had done everything to compensate for her absence. I'd hardly had to live by any rules. There had been no boundaries, no expectations. I was Michael O'Malley's daughter. And I'd gotten into a lot of trouble as a teen. My college years had been nothing but parties and frivolities. Maybe my father should've expected more from me—maybe then I wouldn't feel like I was doomed to fail.

Maybe we are all doomed to fail and nothing prepared us for that.

"Enough, Quinn," I said aloud as I entered the blue guest room and flipped on the light. "No more melancholia. If you can't handle that, then maybe you need to stop drinking. Or go on a cleanse."

"Maybe you should get a cat, and stop talking to yourself."

Chapter Eight

I WHIRLED as a scream lodged in my throat. Forgetting that my ankle was tender, I put weight on it and nearly fell over, but I managed to catch myself.

"What the fuck?" I demanded, a hand to my chest. "You can't go breaking into people's houses!"

Barrett Campbell smiled. "I didn't break in. I had the code. And a set of keys. And I walk silently."

"How?"

"Flynn taught me how to creep—"

"Not *that*. I mean, how did you get a set of keys and the code?"

She waved an elegant hand. "Not important." Her hazel gaze dropped to my torn hose and she frowned. "You okay?"

"Fine," I said in a clipped tone. "What the hell are you doing here?"

"Here? In your house—"

"Stop," I said through gritted teeth. I seethed with anger, felt it prickle under my skin, burning me from the inside out. "You can't be here. I don't want to see you."

She blinked and straightened. "I came because you refuse to return my phone calls."

"My right." Whirling, I tried to shut her out, thinking that if I didn't see her face, I would be able to stand firm. I wanted to escape to the bathroom and lock the door.

Before I knew it, Barrett dodged around me and got in my face. She bit her lip, and she stumbled, her gait uneven.

While Sasha had been healing from burns, Barrett had been bedridden, her body healing from a shattered hip and knee. She didn't wear heels anymore. Heels pronounced her limp.

"Shit," she breathed. "Sometimes I forget…"

My rage tempered into a rolling boil. "I never forget." I wasn't talking about her pain, but my own. And Sasha's. What he—we'd—lived through.

"Please, Quinn," she begged, hazel eyes beseeching. "Can't we sit and talk?"

I paused, my gaze sliding over her head to stare at the wall. Thinking. "Meet me in the den. I need to change."

She nodded and lifted a hand as if to touch me but thought better of it. Barrett walked out of the bedroom, the sounds of her footsteps nonexistent as she walked along the wooden floors.

Before I changed, I washed my knee. The scrape wasn't deep. Purely superficial. I pulled on a comfortable pair of sweats and a warm sweater. It was chilly; the heat was on the lowest setting because it was a large house, and I didn't feel like cranking it just for me.

My slippered feet tracked down the hallway. I held onto the bannister, slowly taking the stairs, as much to give my ankle a rest as to prepare myself. I'd put off speaking to Barrett for nearly a year.

She'd made herself at home on the couch, a glass of

Scotch in her hands. The fireplace was still on, and it turned her auburn hair to molten copper.

I'd once been jealous of her.

Maybe I was still jealous of her.

But I loved her like the sister I'd never had and family was hard to come by.

Her eyes watched me as I made my way to the liquor cart and poured myself a small glass of Bushmills from the crystal decanter. It seemed I was running on liquor fumes and adrenaline.

That cleanse really did need to start tomorrow.

I took a seat in one of the plush chairs across from her, a coffee table in between us. Half the time, it felt like Barrett and I were adversaries. She would have to speak first, and I wasn't going to make this easier for her.

"He went to Russia," she said, lifting the glass of Scotch to her lips. "But I don't know if he's still there."

"So he hasn't…"

She shook her head. "No, Quinn. I haven't heard from him."

I stared into my glass and let out a shaky breath. "Why? Why did he leave?" I looked up at her, willing her to explain the man I loved, the man I didn't completely understand—because he hadn't let me in. Not all the way. There were things he'd shared with me that he hadn't shared with Barrett. And yet, they shared other things. Things I still, to this day, didn't comprehend. Barrett and Sasha's relationship was complicated. It wasn't friendship —it was more. It wasn't lovers—it was less.

Barrett's finger traced the rim of the crystal glass. "He couldn't—He needed to go, Quinn. He needed to find a way to be, just him. He didn't leave you. Well, yes, he did. But he left himself, too. Does that make any sort of sense?"

I nodded, my gritty, tired eyes filling with tears. "I

just… Why did you stay with Flynn? You lived through your own horrors." Once upon a time, Barrett had been kidnapped by the leader of the Russian mafia. Her time with him was something she rarely discussed, but Sasha knew all about it because he'd been second in command. He'd sworn Barrett his allegiance, betraying his leader and oldest friend. He'd sworn Barrett allegiance because he'd fallen in love with her.

"I stayed with Flynn because I had Sasha. He understood, even when Flynn couldn't. Flynn loved me through it, despite not being there. Sasha was *there.*"

I laughed, but it was bitter. "Sasha saved your marriage."

Barrett's lips trembled. "He did. At a great cost to himself. And then he found you."

"He left me." It was a lingering pain, like a phantom limb that tingled and throbbed in the middle of the night, waking you from a sound sleep. "And I don't know if I'll ever forgive him for that."

"I know," she said quietly.

"He told me all we had was dead and that I should move on and be happy."

"I don't think—I don't think he's coming back, Quinn. I think the Sasha we both love is gone."

A dead weight settled in my chest. The last of my hope shriveled and crumbled like a rose in winter.

"More whiskey?" Barrett asked with a tragic smile.

"Bring the bottle," I stated, finally letting the tears I'd been holding in escape. Maybe then I'd begin to feel lighter; maybe then I'd have a chance of finding happiness.

Maybe then I'd start to believe the lies I told myself.

Chapter Nine

"ARE YE KIDDING ME?" came a burly, raspy, Scottish voice.

I cracked an eyelid to find weak winter sunlight in my face—and Flynn Campbell looming over me. "How did you get—"

"Please," he stated, waving his hand.

"Right, you're *the* Flynn Campbell. A man who can walk through walls and charm the pants off all women."

"Hopefully not all women," came Barrett's throaty croak. She'd passed out in a chair the night before, legs dangling over the arm.

"Not anymore, hen," Flynn stated with assurance. He went to his wife's side and held out his hand to her. She grasped it and sat up, groaning. I didn't even bother trying to move. I was in a state of pre-hangover, supine on the couch.

"I think I'm still drunk," Barrett said as she poked at her face. "Feels numb."

"Need omelette," I muttered.

"Ohhhh, I could go for that. Maybe some pancakes. Who's cooking?" Barrett asked.

I raised my eyebrows. "Don't look at me. I don't cook." We both glanced at Flynn.

"You think I cook?" he demanded, finally unraveling the gray scarf from around his neck.

"I cooked. Once upon a time." Barrett removed her legs from the arm of the chair and put them on the floor. She swayed and brought her hand to her head. "Damn, this is worse than morning sickness."

A pang of regret blasted through me, clearing away the last bit of liquor. I stood up quickly. "I'll call out for breakfast."

"Ah, lass," Flynn began as he walked over to the window. He hiked back the drapes to reveal a torrential snowstorm. It was white. Everywhere.

"You drove over here in this weather?" Barrett asked her husband.

He shrugged. "I had to make sure you were both still standing. I can see now that you weren't."

Barrett looked at me. "Do you have eggs?"

I nodded.

"And cheese?"

"Ah, I don't—"

"Help me," Barrett said to Flynn, reaching out her hand. He was by her side in an instant and another one of those pangs shot through my stomach nearly crippling me. Five years together, three children, countless near-death experiences, and they were solid. More than solid. Like two trees that had grown together, needing each other to live.

I thought I'd had that. With Sasha.

"Follow me," I said gruffly, startling the moment of intimacy. I didn't wait to see if they were behind me. Barrett went to the refrigerator and pulled open the silver door. She crouched and peered, rummaged around.

I moved to the cabinet that held the bag of coffee.

While the pot was brewing, Flynn stood at the island while Barrett tossed random ingredients onto the counter.

"I need a mixing bowl and a frying pan," she commanded.

"You would've made a sexy chef," Flynn said to her.

She blew him a kiss.

"Oh God," I muttered, pulling out the items she'd requested. "I don't know if I'm going to hurl because of the booze or because you guys are nauseating."

"Sorry," Barrett said. She set an onion on the cutting board and grabbed a knife and got down to business.

"So," Flynn said, his eyes landing on the brewing dark coffee before coming back to me. "Did you make peace?"

"Ask her," Barrett said. She didn't take her gaze off the onion; her eyes were suspiciously watery.

I gripped the edge of the white granite countertop. "Yes. Peace. Of sorts. I'm still angry."

"But not at me," Barrett said. "Right?" She looked at me for confirmation.

"No," I said quietly. "Not at you."

"Does that mean you're finally ready to set foot in Scotland again?" Flynn asked, a wry grin on his lips. "The lads would be happy to see you."

"Which lads?" I asked, a slight smile appearing.

"Any and all," Flynn said.

"How are the boys?" I asked.

"Raising hell," Barrett said before Flynn could get in a word. "Hawk is almost five and already chasing anything in a skirt."

"Campbell men," Flynn boasted.

Barrett snorted and rolled her eyes at me. Flynn caught the motion and laughed.

"And the twins?"

"Mimicking everything Hawk does," Flynn said.

"I wonder when I have to start dying my hair," Barrett joked. "Three boys under the age of five. It's an insane asylum."

"One you wouldn't trade," Flynn stated. "Admit it."

"I've missed a lot. Haven't I?" I asked, feeling more sober than I wanted to.

"S'okay," Barrett murmured. "Things have been hard."

"How is Duncan? And Ramsey?" I asked after Flynn's surrogate brothers to change the subject and clear the emotion in my throat.

"Duncan is good. Trying to convince Ash to have another baby, but she's steadfastly holding out," Barrett said. "Ramsey is…" She looked at Flynn as she dropped a square of butter into the heated pan.

"Ramsey's in Dallas."

I blinked. "Texas?"

Flynn nodded.

"Why? What happened to Jane?" The last I knew, Flynn's youngest surrogate brother had been headed to the altar with a young British aristocrat.

"She lied to him about some things he found unforgivable," Flynn said, voice hard. "And so she went back to England, and Ramsey went to Dallas."

"What's in Dallas?" I asked in confusion.

Barrett and Flynn exchanged a look. "SINS business," Flynn said finally.

"Ah. Got it." I knew of their political affiliations, but I didn't keep up with it. That was their concern.

"So," Barrett said, scooping up a handful of onions and tossing them into the pan. They crackled and cooked, releasing their sweet aroma into the kitchen. "Are you coming to Dornoch?"

"Not for a while," I said.

"Come on," Barrett begged. "It would be so great to have you—"

"My father left me his business," I blurted out.

They both looked at me, mouths agape.

I nodded. "Yeah, exactly. And until I can pull it together and figure out how not to destroy his company, I won't be going anywhere. Not for a while." I looked at the pan. "I don't know a lot about cooking, but you might want to stir those onions."

Chapter Ten

THE SNOW CONTINUED to come down, paving everything white. The three of us ate breakfast in the kitchen, laughing, and catching up. I couldn't remember the last time I'd shared a meal at that table. Maybe when my mom was still alive. But after she passed, family dinners happened once a week, on Sundays, and always in the expansive dining room or at one of my father's favorite restaurants. None of us wanted to be haunted by my mother's memory, despite the fact that my mother's taste was reflected in the paint colors and the furniture. My father adamantly refused to redecorate the house.

"Yoohoo," Barrett said, waving her hand in front of my face.

Clutching my mug of hot coffee in my hands, I looked at her and smiled. "May I help you?"

"I asked if you were going to postpone going into your father's office." She got up from the table and scooped up our empty plates. After rinsing them, she placed them in the dishwasher.

"I think it's a good idea," Flynn said, pulling out his

phone. He tapped the screen and then showed it to me. The weather app was open, and it showed snow for the next three hours as the temperature continued to drop.

Sighing, I set the cup down and curled my leg underneath my body. "I guess I don't really have a choice. It's not a good idea to drive." I raised an eyebrow. "So I guess that means you both are here for the time being?"

"Ah ha! My plan worked," Barrett teased. She closed the dishwasher door and then came back to sit down. Rubbing her temple, she winced. Guess the hangover was in full throttle.

I felt okay, but I needed to brush my teeth and shower.

"We should call the boys," Barrett said with a look at Flynn.

"You mean the nannies, and find out if the house is still standing," he remarked.

Barrett shook her head. "Girls. Girls would've been so much easier. Why did you give me boys?"

"Me?" Flynn's mouth dropped open.

"And that's my cue," I said, rising and taking my cup of coffee with me. I'd been around them enough to know their banter was some form of foreplay. They couldn't help it, and at one time, I didn't envy it, because I'd had something similar. They didn't mean to shove their happiness in my face, nor did I expect them to hide it from me.

They didn't even notice when I escaped the kitchen. The sounds of their heatless debate followed me as I walked down the hallway. But before I decided to head upstairs, I stopped in front of the closed door of my father's home office. I hadn't gone in there in weeks. Not since he'd been moved to hospice. He'd spent many nights of my childhood working from home. A steadfast workaholic, he had still somehow been around. Because Michael O'Malley had always chosen his family.

I'd been able to count on my father in ways I'd never been able to count on anyone.

Opening the door, I caught the spicy scent that belonged to my father's favorite aftershave. I breathed in the smell as I stepped fully into his home office. After shutting the door, I leaned against it and closed my eyes, letting memories wash over me.

The room was a true gentleman's retreat. Large stone fireplace, comfortable leather Chesterfield, gargantuan dark wood desk. The only piece of furniture that was worn and tired was the leather office chair. It had been a part of this office for the last fifteen years. It was torn in the seat and well-loved. I had sat in it as a child, letting my feet dangle. Now, as an adult, my feet hit the floor. Bracing my hands on the desk, I rolled closer to my father's computer. A keyword protected MacAir.

I woke up the screen and then typed the password. Our birth years, starting with my father's, ending with mine. The screen came to life. It was clean and organized, everything labeled. My eyes scanned the many folders, and already I felt overwhelmed.

No matter the weather tomorrow, I had to go to the office. I had to take my place at the head of my father's company, show my face, and commit. I'd been a wild child growing up, and it had taken me forever to settle. But when I committed to something, I went full throttle, not stopping until I achieved it.

Maybe that was why my father had given me the company.

I'd be damned if I failed.

"I can do this," I whispered. "I *will* do this."

I put the computer to sleep and stood up. For the first time since my father died, I didn't feel so alone, so bereft. Still, the house was too big for just one person. Who knew what Jessica planned on doing when she returned to Boston. If she ever did. She was a young, beautiful, wealthy widow. She might decide to travel. Or remarry. *God.* The idea of her remarrying soon after my father passed made me sick to my stomach.

Some people were meant to go through life with someone by their side. I wasn't one of them. But I was strong enough to do it on my own. I didn't need anyone.

Booming laughter echoed down the hall, muted behind the closed door of the office. I smiled. I guess I did have people.

As I left the office, I heard my cell phone ring. I'd left it in the den and quickly went to grab it. I looked down at the name flashing across the screen. A surge of anger hit me square in the chest.

"Well, it's about fucking time," I snapped.

Chapter Eleven

"Quinn," my brother said. "Please."

"I've been trying to get ahold of you for weeks. *Weeks.* Where are you, Sean? On a mountain top herding goats?"

He paused and sighed. "I'm in London."

"London? What's in London?"

"Adriana has family here. We've been crashing with them."

"All this time?"

My brother had left Boston almost a year ago. He'd come back briefly after my father's diagnosis, but Sean…he wasn't like other people. He had trouble connecting. And so he'd left soon after he realized I would be here. Be here in Boston to hold everything together. That had never been me, but my father's wife couldn't be a stronghold. It was up to me. And I resented it.

"Quinn, I'm sorry," he said. Sean sounded contrite, but I didn't know if he said it because he was truly sorry or because he thought it was what I wanted to hear.

"The will was read yesterday," I said quietly. "He left you a monetary inheritance."

"I don't care about any of that." His tone was gruff.

"He took care of Jessica."

"What did he give you, Quinn?" he asked in curiosity.

"The business."

My brother fell silent.

"Good," he said finally.

It was easy to detect the relief in his voice. "You didn't want it, did you?"

"No," he admitted. "I never wanted it. I'm not cut out to run Dad's business."

"And you think I am?" I snapped. Rage rolled through my veins. "I don't know a damn thing about any of this! What if I fail?"

"You won't."

"How do you know?"

"Because you're Quinn O'Malley. And anytime you've wanted to achieve something, you have."

"I didn't have any drive in college. You know that."

"You're not a kid anymore."

"Why did you have to leave, Sean?" I asked.

Why does everyone I love leave me?

"Because I—I don't know. I was selfish."

"Am," I corrected. "You still are selfish."

"Yeah. I guess I am."

"Why don't you sound guiltier about it?"

"Why should I live a life of obligation?" he countered.

"Our father—"

"He got sick, Quinn. He got sick and didn't tell us until it was too late."

"So you left because you were angry at him? You wanted to what? Punish him? Punish me?"

"I wanted—Hell, I didn't know what I wanted. I just knew staying in Boston, watching him die was killing me."

"Like I said, selfish."

We both paused, momentarily retreating. Reflecting, maybe. Or waiting to strike again. "He asked for you," I told him. "Our father looked at me, with tears in his eyes, and asked for you. I called you, but you didn't answer. I held the phone in one hand, waiting for you to answer and you never did."

I swallowed and got it together.

"His hand went cold in mine, Sean. It went cold in mine, because I was there when he slipped away."

"And that's your last memory of him," he said, his voice detached. "My last memory is of him laughing because I told him a stupid joke. I left because I needed to remember him that way."

"Goodbye, Sean." I hung up on the only blood family I had left and curled my fingers around my cell phone.

Death was hardest on those left behind.

I heard someone shift behind me and without turning around, I asked, "How much did you hear?"

Barrett sighed. "Fuck."

Looking at her over my shoulder, I sent her a wobbly smile. I refused to cry for the brother I didn't understand, who was very much alive. Yet I mourned for him too. I grieved his absence and wished he were there with me. Because as much as I hated him for being a selfish prick, he was still my brother. We were Irish twins, so close in age we were at times more friends than siblings.

But we hadn't been that close in a long, long time.

"I've got a remedy for this," Barrett said.

"Please don't say liquor," I begged. "I've had enough of that the last few days."

"Not liquor." She turned back in the direction of the kitchen, and I reluctantly followed her. Flynn was sitting at the kitchen table, scrolling through his phone.

"Sit," she instructed, pointing to the kitchen table chair.

I sat.

She brought over a mixing bowl, sugar, vanilla, salt, and milk. She dumped all the ingredients into the bowl and whisked them quickly.

"What are you—?"

"Wait," Barrett said with a grin. She grabbed the bowl and whisk and dashed for the patio door. The door slid open, and a blast of cold air shot through the kitchen as Barrett disappeared outside.

I looked at Flynn who grinned and shrugged. A moment later, Barrett was back inside, shutting the door, teeth chattering. She whisked a few more times and then set the bowl in front of me.

"Voilà," she said with a smile. "Snowcream."

I glanced down at the fluffy white peaks, and I started to laugh. "Snowcream."

Barrett moved around the kitchen, opening a few drawers before finding the spoons. She handed one to me and one to Flynn. "Well, dig in. Before it melts."

The three of us plowed our spoons into the concoction. I stuck a spoonful in my mouth and shook my head. "Unreal," I muttered.

"Right?" She beamed. "I don't get to do this very often. Not really enough snow in Dornoch."

"Your kids are missing out," I said. I clutched the spoon in my hand. "Thank you."

I wasn't thanking her for the snowcream, and she knew it when she replied, "You're welcome."

We ate the rest in silence. I knew they'd have to leave eventually, but for the moment, I was glad for their presence.

"This house is too big for one person," I voiced.

"Thinking about selling it?" Flynn asked.

"Not mine to sell. Dad gave the house to Jessica." I shrugged. "I've been staying in the pool house." I gestured to the patio door with my chin. "I think I'm glad he didn't leave me the house. Now, it's not my problem. But I just— want a clean start. Do you really ever get those?"

Flynn and Barrett exchanged a look.

"Yeah," I said with a sigh. "I get it."

Part of the reason I was so angry with my brother was because I was jealous. Jealous that he decided to say "screw it" and fly across the world, shirk duties and obligations.

I was jealous he chose to act like a child when I had to be an adult. Adults thought about things like responsibilities and legacies. I'd grown up, I realized, and I wasn't sure how I felt about that.

Chapter Twelve

The snowstorm stopped early the next morning and Barrett and Flynn took advantage of the break. They wanted to get back to Dornoch, back to their three young sons. Before she left, Barrett embraced me tightly and said in my ear, "When I call, you answer."

I nodded, relief sweeping through me. Life had been topsy-turvy, and I hadn't felt peace in a long time. Being at odds with Barrett had only made things worse. The past would never really be behind us, not when it always showed up in the present. But, you had to find a way to keep moving forward.

"Call if you need anything," Flynn added. "If I can lend any sort of help with the business transition, you let me know."

"Thank you," I murmured, feeling humble and grateful.

An hour later, I was dressed in warm clothes and comfortable boots. Donovan was on his way, and I had plans to make it into the office. I had no time to waste. This was now my company, and I needed to oversee it.

Donovan arrived and I bundled myself into a thick bubble coat. For a girl who normally looked like a Ralph Lauren model, at the moment, I was sporting the L.L. Bean look. Ah, if only my father could see me now. That brought a genuine smile to my lips.

"You're looking well," Donovan remarked, holding the car door open for me.

"I'm feeling well," I told him. I took his offered hand and slid into the car. Resting the travel mug of coffee between my legs, I yanked off my hat and gloves so I wouldn't overheat.

The door closed and then Donovan was back up front, putting the car into drive. "How did you weather the storm?"

"Which one?" I quipped. I told him about Barrett's surprise visit, our making amends over liquor, and then Flynn showing up the next morning to make sure we were both still standing after our fight.

"I'm glad for you, Quinn. They were good friends to you and Michael trusted them."

"Yeah, because Dad did business with Flynn."

Dad never went into business with someone he couldn't trust. It was a good mantra. That wasn't to say my father hadn't been corrupt. I had no doubt that he was. We had ties to the IRA for crying out loud.

Flynn's uncle in Belfast had been a lifelong friend to my father.

Twisted small political mafia world, right?

My father had trusted Sasha because Flynn trusted Barrett, and Barrett and Sasha were like…well, there wasn't a name for what they meant to each other. Thoughts of Sasha drifted through my head.

I sighed.

"You okay?" Donovan asked.

Shaking my head, I lifted the travel mug of coffee to my lips. "Fine," I said before taking a sip. The coffee was lukewarm so it didn't scald, and it was more cream than coffee. Truth? I hated coffee, but I couldn't exist without the caffeine.

The drive to the office took longer than usual due to the icy roads. Though a plow had come through and cleared away the snow on the main roads, the salt would need some time to work. Most people hated the cold Boston winters. They were wet and dark. I loved them, though. To me, they were familiar and when summer hit, it made it feel like I'd really earned the nice weather. Summers were spent on Martha's Vineyard, eating lobster and riding bikes around the island. Some of my best memories came from those summers. Couldn't have summer without winter, though.

We took it slow and steady, but finally we made it to the office. I peered through the window of the car. The building was dark.

"This might've been a bad idea," I remarked. "It's the day after a snowstorm. No one is in there."

"Best time to go in," Donovan said. "No watchful eyes."

I sighed. "Valid point." I got out of the car, gathering my hat and gloves. I didn't need to put them on since I was only going a few feet. Trying the glass door, I discovered it was locked. I reached into my coat pocket and pulled out my keys. Fiddling with the ring, I found the set that unlocked the office. I shoved the door open and turned halfway around to give a thumbs up to Donovan. The door automatically locked behind me.

O'Malley Properties took up the entire building. The lobby normally had a security guard and desk attendant, but at the moment, it was quiet. I headed to the elevator and rode it to the top floor. All the other floors belonged to the architects and accountants. I'd been to those floors once or twice when my father dragged me on a tour, but when I'd come to visit him, I always went right to the top —his office—and then we'd leave the building to grab lunch at one of the many restaurants nearby.

I was kicking myself for not taking a more active interest in his business, but how was I to know?

The elevator doors opened to reveal a dark and quiet floor. I flipped on the lights and marveled at the view. One entire wall was made of glass, and I could see the city which was white and quiet. Very few cars were on the road. It only reinforced my idiocy that I'd decided to trek out of my warm home. I walked passed my father's secretary's neat and orderly desk and turned the handle of my father's office. It was locked.

Shaking my head, I took my keys out again and unlocked the door. The room was just like the home study office. Same type of furniture, same scent. But there was a subtle difference. His home office had been where he could take a moment and breathe. Here, in this office, my father had been king of the city. Here, he'd been larger than life. At home, he'd just been my father.

A sob caught in my throat. I shoved it down. Shrugging out of my coat, I walked to the desk and took a seat in the office chair. There was no computer on the desk—it was at home.

"What the hell am I doing here?" I muttered as I opened the center drawer of his desk. I expected to find pens and paperclips, sticky notes and other office supplies. Instead, I found an envelope with my name scrawled across it.

"No," I whispered, lifting it from the drawer and holding it in my hands. I knew it was a letter. Had to be.

And I wasn't ready to read the words from my deceased father.

Coward.

I could almost hear my father's low chuckle.

Taking a deep breath, I tore the letter open.

Chapter Thirteen

QUINN,

Forgive me.

Love, Dad

I stared at the letter. Those three lines and I had no words. Utterly speechless. I'd been expecting a long letter, at least a page, where my father explained to me why he'd given me his business, why he had such faith in me, why he loved me and believed in me. Instead, all I got was a lousy *forgive me.*

What. The. Fuck.

Tossing aside the letter in disgust, I got up from the chair and wandered over to the maple wall-to-wall shelves. On one of them rested two crystal glasses and a glass decanter. Scooping up a glass and the decanter, I took them back to the desk. I poured myself a hefty glass and threw it back. I poured another, raised it to the ceiling, said nothing, and then slid it back.

When I finished my drink, I stared into the empty glass and then hurled it against the wall. It shattered on impact.

"Easy," a voice said behind me.

I whirled to face the open door. A tall, broad cop in uniform stood in the doorway, hand resting on his holster. My eyes narrowed. "May I help you, Officer?"

"Yes." He took a step toward me, his eyes darting to the wall behind me. "You can show me some ID."

"Excuse me?"

"The silent alarm went off," he explained, his tone still mild, brown eyes on mine.

Shit.

"My name is Quinn O'Malley and this is my fath—I own this building." I squared my shoulders and then I moved toward my purse which was slung across the back of the office chair.

"Hey," he began.

"I'm getting my ID," I said, looking at him. "Okay?"

His nod was curt. I went to my bag and unzipped it. Digging around, I searched for my wallet. It wasn't there.

I closed my eyes. I'd changed purses when I'd gone to the wake and the lawyer's office and hadn't moved my wallet back into my regular purse.

"Ah, Officer," I said. "It seems I've left my wallet at home."

"So you can't prove who you are. I'm afraid I'm going to need you to—"

"Wait! My keys! I have keys to the building." I rifled through my coat and pulled them out to show him. The cop didn't look at all impressed.

"I'm going to need to take you down to the station—

just until I can prove your identity and that you weren't trespassing."

"Trespassing!" I shouted. "I showed you the keys."

"Can't validate them, Ms. O'Malley."

"Listen"—I glanced at his nametag—"Officer Grimaldi. My name is Quinn O'Malley. My father was Michael O'Malley, and he left me his company." I gestured to the office I was standing in. "This is all mine, bucko."

Officer Grimaldi reached for his dispatch transmitter on his shoulder, pressed a button, and said, "I've got a hostile trespasser in the O'Malley Properties building. No ID. Bringing her in to validate her identity."

"Wait just a minute—"

"Trespasser seems to be intoxicated and"—he looked at the spot on the wall—"unstable." He signed off and then made a move toward me. "Let's go."

I had just enough Bushmills in my system to be an idiot. "No."

Before I knew it, I had cuffs around my wrists, and I was being led toward the elevators, police station bound.

"Quinn O'Malley, as I live and breathe," Chief Whitcomb said, a wry smile on his ruddy face.

"Thank God!" I jumped up from the uncomfortable bench in the jail cell and went to him. "You came."

"Of course I came." He laughed and reached for his belt. Extracting a key, he had the door open in a moment. "When Grimaldi called and said he had someone claiming to be Quinn O'Malley, and she was acting hostile and inebriated, I knew I had to come see for myself."

I flung my arms around his neck. Chief Whitcomb had saved my ass on more than one occasion when I was a teenager. If it weren't for him, I'd have had my name and face splashed across the news as Michael O'Malley's wild-child daughter.

"Grimaldi's new to the force," he said, leaning back, his arms dropping. "Otherwise he would've recognized you."

"I don't know if that's good or bad."

"Good. All good." He squeezed my shoulder. "Come on, I'll walk you out." He held my hand in his monstrous paw, making me feel like a reckless girl again. He'd come to my father's funeral but not the wake. He was a good man, and I appreciated everything he'd done for me when I was an untamable teenager who'd just lost her mother.

We stopped at the desk, and Chief Whitcomb asked the officer on duty to grab my personal belongings. Once they were handed over, Chief Whitcomb walked me toward the exit as he continued to talk. "Are you going to the mayor's gala?"

Squinting my tired eyes, I rubbed my temple. "When is that?"

"Next weekend."

"Right. I think I remember getting that invitation. Must've slipped my mind." I wasn't in the mood for parties, but when the mayor of the city sent you an invitation to his annual gala, you went. It would be good for business, I thought wryly. "I didn't RSVP. I suppose I could call his office and ask if it's too late."

"I'm sure it wouldn't be." He winked. "Not for Quinn O'Malley."

Laughing, I leaned up to brush a kiss across his cheek. "Tell Officer Grimaldi I want his badge."

When we arrived to the police station doors, we stopped. "Do you really?" he asked. "Because I'll gladly—"

I blinked. "I was teasing. But good to know I have that sort of clout."

He chuckled. "Not many people do."

"Thanks again." I hugged him one last time. The day was sinking into night, and the temperature had dropped again. I climbed into the waiting car and met Donovan's eyes in the rear view mirror.

"Don't say a word," I warned.

And he didn't. But he did let out a chuckle.

Chapter Fourteen

THE NEXT FEW days passed in a blur. More snow hit Boston. I spent most of my time at the house, trying to sift through the many folders and files on my father's computer. Blue prints, contracts, deals in different stages of completion. I ranted at my father while I sat as his desk, clutching a glass of Bushmills, still resentful that his letter hadn't assuaged my feelings of loss and anger. Instead, it had rejuvenated them. His letter had given me no instructions, no roadmap for how I was supposed to fill his size eleven shoes.

I called the mayor's office to let them know I'd be coming to the gala. When his assistant asked if I was bringing a plus one, I forced myself to take a calming breath and say no.

Growling in frustration, I stood up from the computer, my eyes bleary. I needed someone to translate the jargon.

I took a break and headed upstairs to the guest bedroom. I needed something for the mayor's gala but quickly realized that my clothes had started to hang on me.

Grabbing my cell phone, I took a seat on the side of

the bed. I dialed Shannon with one hand while finishing off the rest of my drink. A drink was never far from my hands these days. I wasn't worried, though. I'd been reckless in my teenage years. This…wasn't that. This was, well, existing. Helping me numb out.

It was better than pills, anyway.

Shannon's cell rang and after the third, she picked up. "Quinn? Can you hold on?" Shannon said immediately.

"Sure."

There was shuffling, and then I heard the unmistakable sounds of someone vomiting. A smile crept across my face.

"You there?" Shannon's voice was muffled, like she was speaking through a towel. Probably wiping her mouth.

"I'm here. Thanks for the audio show."

She groaned. "I'm sorry. I puke all the time now. Not just in the mornings."

"Ah," I murmured quietly.

A heavy pause stretched between us.

"So, what's up," she asked with renewed cheer.

"I'm going to the mayor's gala, and none of my dresses will work."

"So you want to go shopping."

"Ya. And definitely hit the spa. I need a day to be pampered."

"That's for sure. Tomorrow?"

Getting up from the bed, I looked toward the window. Fluttery flakes drifted down, landing and sticking. "Tomorrow—but only if the roads are cleared."

The plows had been out working nonstop, it seemed, and still they couldn't keep up with the weather. There had been tons of accidents. Weather, one, city of Boston, zero.

"Are you taking anyone to the gala?" Shannon asked.

"Who would I take?"

"I don't know. Adam."

"I didn't even think of that," I admitted. "That would've been a good idea. But I already told the mayor's office it was just me."

"Do you think…"

"What?" I asked, pulling aside the drapes to stare out into the white.

"Do you think that's always going to be you, Quinn? Wanting to be alone?"

"Life has been pretty good to you, Shannon," I reminded her quietly. "And I—You're gentle and sweet and kind, and you've been there for me. Through it all. Do I want to be alone?" I paused as I thought. "No. No, I don't. But I can't have what I want, so why should I think about settling?"

"That makes sense," she allowed. "But if you don't share yourself with someone, it just feels… It feels like the unhappiness wins. It feels like life is in control of you when you should be in control of your life."

That was such a Shannon thing to say. Shannon who had fallen in love with a boy at sixteen and married him junior year of college. That wasn't the usual. They'd both found a way to grow and change together, at a time when people seemed to do most of their changing. Now, they were expecting a baby. Some people achieved their dreams.

Even if Sasha had stayed and we'd found a way through the hardships, our lives wouldn't have looked like Shannon and Patrick's. You lived a different kind of life when you were the king of the Russian mafia of New York. You lived a different kind of life as the woman who stood by his side.

Though Shannon was my oldest friend and the one closest to my heart, sometimes I felt like we didn't under-stand each other at all. Sometimes, I felt like I had more in common with Barrett. After all, she was the wife of Flynn Campbell, co-leader of the SINS, the Scottish version of the IRA. She'd learned of his sympathies, loved him anyway, and his cause had become her cause. And they'd had kids. Three boys who'd grow up in that life.

"You still there?" came Shannon's voice.

"Yeah, still here."

"I won't bug you about it anymore. I promise."

I smiled even though she couldn't see me. "Yes, you will."

She sighed. "Yes, I will, because I love you."

"I know. And I love you, too. I'll pick you up at ten. Is that okay?"

"Should be fine. If I'm running late it's because I'm throwing my guts up."

I laughed.

"Listen, should I try and not talk about the—"

"No," I cut her off. "You talk about it. You share about it. And please, whatever you do, don't worry about how I feel. I can't…" My throat was tight with emotion and speaking through it was difficult. "I'm so happy for you, Shannon."

"You really are, aren't you?" she whispered, her own voice shaky.

"What kind of friend would I be if I couldn't revel in your joy?"

"You're the best. It's why you're going to be a great godmother."

"Yeah?"

"Yeah."

"I'm going to spoil him or her rotten. You know that."

"I do."

"And I'm going to be so awesome that your kid is going to love me more."

We both laughed.

"I'll see you tomorrow," she said.

Hanging up, I walked over to the bed and fell back onto it. My hands instinctively went to rest on my stomach. I fell asleep and dreamed about blond-haired, blue-eyed babies. Babies I'd never have with Sasha.

Chapter Fifteen

MAYOR BRIGSBY LIVED in a mansion forty-five minutes outside the heart of Boston. He came from old money, so it had only been natural that he'd wound up in politics. Every year, he threw a gala in March. Invitations were coveted and the press wasn't allowed.

I'd been around these types of events my entire life. My father had been a major player in the shaping of Boston. He knew the big guns, and he knew which people to have in his pocket. There was a very good chance my father had cut many a deal that weren't on the books and part of me worried what I would uncover as I dug deeper into his business.

"Holy hotness, Batman!"

I turned and grinned in relief and surprise. "What are *you* doing here?" I asked as I approached Adam. He was dressed in a black suit with a skinny tie and crisp white shirt. His hair was styled in that carefree way that meant he'd spent an hour on it.

His gaze raked down me and then went back up to linger on my newly bobbed hair. In a fit of needing a new identity, I'd chopped off my signature dark locks that I'd worn long my entire life. Now, my hair barely kissed my shoulders.

"God, I'm so loving everything about this right now." His hand gestured up and down before he lunged for me to pull me into a hug. "You're like the anti-Quinn."

I laughed. "How's that now?"

His hand touched my hair. "Such a simple change. And yet you no longer look like a heroine." Adam grinned. "You look like the dark horse, the anti-heroine, if you will."

"Feel free to use me in your next book," I said.

"Only if you promise to read it."

"I don't like romance novels."

"Well, you're an idiot."

I shook my head. Adam wrote romance novels under a female pen name. Not only was he incredibly successful, he had a dedicated cult following. I wondered what his fans would do if they found out their favorite author, the one who gave them risqué fantasies they could escape into, was a hot gay man. Probably worship him even more.

A passing waiter in a tuxedo held a tray of champagne flutes. He stopped in front of us, and with a smile and a thanks, I took a glass. "You never told me why you're here," I reminded him.

"Richard remodeled the mayor's second floor bathroom last year. Richard and Linda are like, BFFs now."

I raised my eyebrows. "Your husband and the mayor's conservative wife are like this?" I crossed my two fingers and held them up.

Adam nodded. "Ever since Richard called her out about a hideous scarf and said she was too young to dress so dumpy, she's been all about him."

"Strange, isn't it?"

"What? Their friendship?"

"Yep."

Adam scoffed and tossed back his champagne. "Richard spent so many years lying, pretending to be something he wasn't, and then when he finally came out, he vowed to always tell the truth."

"I can understand that. He might be—ah—taking it to the extreme, though. If he calls the mayor's wife dumpy."

Adam laughed. "I wish I'd been there to see it."

"Me too."

We laughed together, and I felt lighter than I had in a long time. The champagne bubbles were flowing through my bloodstream. "Where's the food?" I asked, looking around.

"Over—Whoa."

My gaze slid to his face. "Whoa, what?"

"The hottest guy I've ever seen is staring at you."

I rolled my eyes. "You said that at the bar, remember? About Flynn? You need some new material."

"Flynn," he said, turning the name over on his tongue. "He was hot. Like stupid hot. But this guy. I don't know. There's some sort of…animal intensity to him."

"Oh, God, you really are an author." I sighed. "Now you've got me curious."

"Ten o'clock."

Lifting my glass, I slowly swiveled my head.

There he was. In the corner, clutching a tumbler, and staring at me. A shiver of excitement worked its way down my spine. I hadn't felt that in…well, too long. And I decided to have a little fun.

I took a sip of champagne and then, without breaking eye contact, I ran my tongue slowly across my upper lip, pretending to catch a stray drop.

The man's eyes dipped to my mouth and even from far

away, I could tell his gaze darkened, heated. And then he was striding toward me.

"What did you do?" Adam whispered.

I didn't answer him. I couldn't. Because the man with the intense gaze was coming toward me. He was a force—and he seemed to grow larger.

He stopped when he was about a foot away from me. His eyes dipped to my mouth, and he raised his tumbler to his lips. I watched in fascination when the corded column of his throat moved as he swallowed whatever was left in his glass.

His eyes were the color of dark chocolate, and they stared at me, bored into me, giving away nothing.

"Shit weather," he said finally.

I choked on a laugh, surprised by the man's crass language. So at odds with the expensive tuxedo he wore. Custom, of course. "Yes," I agreed readily. Because Boston winters were brutal and this one was no different.

"Do you like Bermuda?"

Blinking, I let out a huff of air. "I don't know. I've never been."

"Want to go?" he asked. His stance was alert, belying the casual delivery of his words.

My smile widened. "Sure."

"Great." Without taking his eyes off me, he handed off his tumbler to a passing waiter. "Let's go."

"Now? With you?" I asked.

The man's eyes slid from me to rest on Adam. "Do you mind if I take your girlfriend to Bermuda?"

Adam let out a laugh. "She's not my girlfriend."

The man's lips twitched and then pulled into a smile. "Well, that is excellent news."

"I doubt that would've stopped you anyway," Adam quipped.

"You're right," the man agreed. "It makes things a hell of a lot easier, though." He held out his arm to me.

"Are you kidding me?" I demanded.

"I never kid."

I rolled my eyes. "Okay, look. I don't know what you thought by coming over here—"

"Excuse me," he interrupted, dropping his arm. "*You're* the one who summoned *me.*"

"How do you figure?"

The man swiped his upper lip with his tongue in an exaggerated gesture. "If that wasn't an invitation, then you're nothing but a rich bitch cock tease."

"You arrogant son of a—"

Before I could land myself in a mess of trouble by launching myself at the stranger who looked at me like I owed him something, Adam stepped in front of me.

"I think you better leave now," he said, tone mild.

The man ran a thumb down the contour of his chiseled cheek. "I think you're right." And with that final announcement, the man turned and left.

Chapter Sixteen

"WHAT A DICK," Adam muttered under his breath.

"Right? Ugh. Men suck."

"Hey!"

"Present company excluded."

"That's better." He smiled. "Should we get another drink?"

"Yes. Immediately. Something stronger than champagne."

He looked at a spot over my shoulder. "Ah, I think we're about to be saved."

I frowned in confusion and turned. Adam's husband was walking toward us, carrying three cocktail glasses. He'd been a server once upon a time, and it still showed in moments like these and at their dinner parties.

"Try this," Richard said without a *hello*. He handed me a glass filled with ice and some sort of plum-colored liquid.

"What is it?" Adam asked, taking another glass from Richard and holding it to his nose.

"Guess."

I took a sip. "Pomegranate something."

"Ohhh," Adam moaned. "That's incredible."

"Linda and I spent all afternoon playing with cocktail recipes."

I chuckled and took another sip. "Linda your new BFF. That's right. Adam filled me in."

Richard shook his head. "All it took was one phone call from her to redesign her upstairs bathroom, and suddenly I'm booked for the next six months."

"So business is good," I said.

He grinned, showing straight, white teeth in his tanned face. Richard was half Puerto Rican, and he had color all year round. Not like the rest of us Bostonians that could pass for Victorian vampires.

"Business is good," Richard repeated.

"Too good," Adam grumbled with feigned annoyance. "We can't book a vacation any time soon."

"Why don't I call back that mystery asshole and ask him to take you to Bermuda."

Richard looked at me and then at Adam. "What did I miss?"

I told him.

Richard's dark brows nearly went into his hairline. "And he's gone?"

"Yeah. Didn't get a name. Not that it matters," I hastened to add. "He was a first-class jerk. And I know jerks."

"He was hot, though," Adam admitted.

"All the jerks are," I pointed out before I could stop myself.

"That's not really true and you know it," Richard said pointedly.

I sighed. "Yeah. Sasha wasn't a jerk. He was...something else."

The conversation halted with awkwardness, and the

three of us sipped on our drinks to try and cover it. Even though Sasha and I had made our home in Manhattan, we'd visited Boston enough. We'd spent time around my friends and family—and they'd all loved him.

He'd left so much emptiness when he'd disappeared.

"Do you think about him?" Richard asked softly, his gaze on the party as if trying to soften the intensity of his question.

"I try not to," I admitted. "It's nearly impossible."

Adam wrapped an arm around me and pulled me into his side, but he didn't say anything. What could he say? That I was better off? That we were all better off? Sasha had survived a terrible childhood, but life had finally broken him. The fire…

After the fire, and the hospital…just as we were getting our footing, he'd left.

Shaking my head, I chased thoughts of him away with a swallow of the pomegranate cocktail.

"Another?" Richard asked.

I shrugged and threw him a masked smile. "Why not?"

The rest of the night passed in a blur of alcohol and trivial conversation. Most of the people at the party had known my father, so I spent hours with a fake smile on my face, telling stories of my childhood, spinning tales to cover my brother's absence.

By 2 AM, the party was in full-swing, but I'd had enough. I'd talked to everyone I needed to, even gabbing with the mayor and the police chief. Adam and Richard saw me to the door and with a few hugs, I left. Donovan was waiting and I climbed into the car, sighing in relief.

I'd gone through a gamut of emotions—rejecting them, owning them. They exhausted me, but it was better than being numb. Or so I told myself.

"How was the party?" Donovan asked, putting the car into gear.

"Good. I think." I pinched the bridge of my nose. "The beginning was good." It had been fun. Until that asshole had derailed my mood. I'd felt…*off* since our encounter.

"Meet anyone interesting?"

"Nope," I lied. That man *had* been interesting, intriguing. But I hadn't liked how he'd made me feel. Off kilter, swept along in a rushing river, struggling to keep my head above water. And I hadn't liked how he'd spoken to me.

"Did I tell you that I like the hair?"

I smiled. "Yes. When you picked me up."

"Well, I do. You look…"

"What?"

"Devilish. And up to no-good."

Kicking off my heels, I leaned back against the leather seat. "I don't have the energy for no-good."

"Maybe you should find the energy," he suggested.

"Donovan," I began, "are you trying to tell me to revert back to my wild-child days?"

"No."

"Good."

"I'm telling you to become a wild woman." His eyes met mine in the rearview mirror, and he winked.

I laughed. "You do realize I think of you as an uncle."

"Take it from me, lass. A lot can be settled with a good roll in the sack."

"Spoken like a man," I teased.

"Spoken like a woman," he shot back. "He was the only one strong enough to make a woman out of you."

Sasha talk. Twice in one night. Nope. Had to shut that down immediately.

"I'm uncomfortable with this line of conversation."

"Good. You need to be uncomfortable, Quinn. It's the only way you'll grow."

"Fine," I snapped. "I'll go out tomorrow night and pick up a stranger. Happy?"

He sighed. "You know that's not what I'm suggesting."

"It's not? Then I must've heard you wrong. When are people going to stop offering me unsolicited advice?"

"When you take it. Or"—he turned down my street—"you tell them to feck off."

Chapter Seventeen

I WAS GETTING OLD, I thought as I set my house keys on the front entrance table. Parties where I had to dress up, drink, make lively conversation, and flirt…I was over it. Shaking my head, I sighed. I hadn't seen that coming. I used to love parties, the glitz, the glam. None of that seemed to matter anymore.

The den was dark, and I fumbled around for the lamp. Warm light bathed the dark wood end table and the couch. I sat down, leaned back, and let out a tired sigh.

"Quinn," a dark, raspy voice said, coming out of the darkness.

"Ah!" I yelled, my eyes searching for the occupant of the room. "What the hell?"

"Easy."

"Why do people think they can break into my house in the middle of the night? Who does that?" I demanded.

There was a pause. "Who else has been sneaking into your house?"

"None of your damn business," I muttered. "What the hell are you doing here?"

The shadow shifted, showing a gray pant leg, though his face remained in shadow. "Checking in on you."

"Orders from Sasha?" I asked, my tone snide.

Another pause and then, "No. Not from him. Haven't heard from him in months."

I shook my head, trying to push away the hurt. A part of me hoped Sasha still cared enough about me to keep tabs. That was the sick part of me. The hopeful part of me. The part of me that needed to die. Otherwise I'd never move on.

"What do you want, Dimitri?" I asked.

"For starters? A glass of vodka would be nice."

I waved my hand toward the liquor cart. "Help yourself."

He got up and moved to the liquor cart without stumbling or bumping into anything. Dimitri was a shadow with cat eyes, apparently.

"*Krasnyy* is doing well." His Russian accent was mild, just like Sasha's.

"So that's why you're here."

"We have to capitalize on the success—"

"Not interested," I said, my tone harsh. "I helped out with the last campaign because the model the magazine hired was too busy sleeping off a coke binge."

"Quinn—"

"No, Dimitri. Get someone else."

Krasnyy was Sasha's Lower East Side vodka lounge and a few years ago, he'd begun to manufacture his own *Krasnyy* line of vodka. It wasn't for sale anywhere except at his club. To celebrate the launch of the product, *Krasnyy* and Sasha had been featured in a magazine. An ad had been attached to the article—a woman sitting in a glass cube, filled with vodka. The original model had flaked, and I'd replaced her at the last minute. After the photo shoot,

Sasha had locked us in the back office of his club and fucked me across the desk.

"No one will do the job like you," Dimitri said, startling me out of my past.

I snorted. "Flattery won't work. I want nothing to do with the lounge or the ads."

"What can I do to change your mind?"

"Nothing."

"He signed over the club to you," he said, his voice soft, dangerous.

I closed my eyes and shook my head. The two men I'd loved most in this world had both left me and signed away their legacies to me. I forced my lids open and stared hard at Dimitri. "Did he, now?"

Dimitri hesitated and then nodded.

"Sell it."

"What? You can't mean—"

"Sell the lounge," I commanded again. "Burn it for all I care."

"You of all people should not mention burning."

I swallowed, suddenly assaulted with the memory of singed flesh. He'd been so beautiful, his eyes the color of a frigid lake in winter, his Slavic cheekbones prominent. And his body. His body had made me burn with need. After the accident, he couldn't stand to have me touch him, look at him. We'd slept in separate beds for months, and then one night, he'd come to me scarred, burnt, bitter, and he made love to me like he'd never get to again. From that night on, we'd shared a bed again, and every night he made love to me. We didn't talk about the past anymore, and when he'd grimace in pain, we both ignored it. We'd tried to sweep it under the pile of ashes, both wanting to move forward. At least I had. Apparently he couldn't move forward, so he'd left.

"Get out of here, Dimitri. And don't come back."

Dimitri set his empty glass of vodka aside and stood. "I won't stop checking in on you." He buttoned the jacket of his suit coat and moved toward the door. I didn't even hear him leave.

I cursed Boston, wanting to do what Sasha had done and leave my old life behind. But you didn't leave responsibility; you didn't leave loved ones behind.

"Your eleven o'clock is here," my father's secretary said through the phone.

"Thanks." I hung up and stood. I brushed a hand down my black skirt, but I knew I looked impeccable and professional. The red heels I'd worn on the first official day to the office gave me more height and attitude. Every time I thought I couldn't do it, couldn't be Quinn O'Malley, those shoes reminded me I could kick some serious ass. And do it in heels.

The door to my father's office opened, and a tall man in a black suit entered. His chocolate brown eyes were on me, dipping down my body as he slowly shut the door.

"You!" I spat, immediately recognizing the asshole from the mayor's gala.

He grinned. "Me."

"Get out."

His grin widened. "We have an appointment." He sauntered toward me, eating up the space of the room as he held out his hand. "I'm afraid we got off to a bad start. Ori Abruzzo."

I looked at his hand and didn't take it. "Did you know who I was the night of the gala?"

"Yes. You haven't shaken my hand."

"I don't intend to. Excuse me, but I'm very busy." It was the truth—I was trying to sort through my father's files. I needed to hire a personal assistant who spoke real estate jargon. Maybe Flynn could offer a recommendation.

Abruzzo dropped his hand, but his smile remained in place. "I'm trying to apologize. I'd just flown in from out of town, I was jet lagged, exhausted, and annoyed that my date canceled on me at the last minute. I don't take rejection well."

"You called me a rich bitch cock tease."

"Like I said, I was in fine form that night." He sighed. "My mother would kill me if she knew I'd spoken to a woman that way."

"Really?" I picked up the office phone. "What's her number?"

Chapter Eighteen

ORI ABRUZZO THREW BACK his head and laughed. "Mama would love you," he said, dark eyes appraising.

I couldn't say I was immune to it. It had been so long since a man had looked at me with anything except pity. I didn't like Ori Abruzzo. He was an ass, confident and assured. But he was handsome, and when he wanted to be, charming.

I put the phone back in its receiver. "Why would she like me? Because I'd be able to keep you in line?"

"Something like that." His smile remained on his face. "So listen, can I take you to lunch?"

"It's eleven o'clock in the morning. And I thought you wanted to have a business meeting?"

He leaned over and pressed his hands to my desk. "I've had this meeting scheduled with your father for months. When I heard about his health... I'm sorry. For your loss."

I nodded curtly, accepting his sympathy.

"I'd like to make amends for how I treated you the other night, but I'd also like to discuss the business venture I had planned."

Could I do business with someone I didn't like?

I glanced at the photo of my father, which rested on my desk. I'd brought it from home so that any time I felt like I was losing my way or my mind, I could look at it. It was as if he was silently saying, "Keep going. Don't be afraid."

"Fine. We can go to lunch," I said, walking out from behind the desk and heading for the coat rack. Before I could grab my coat, Abruzzo was already there, holding it out for me to slip into.

"You have no idea how glad I am that you're finally giving me a chance." He rested his hands on my shoulders and then dropped them.

Turning, I buttoned my coat. "Hmmm. We'll see about that. We're going to one of my spots."

Abruzzo inclined his head. "Fine, but we're going to one of my favorite spots for dessert."

I arched an eyebrow. "A hotel room?"

He chuckled. "If the lady is so inclined."

The idea of hate sex suddenly appealed to me. "Depends how lunch goes."

Abruzzo opened the door and waited for me to leave first.

"Guess you can be chivalrous."

"You're going to make me work for it, aren't you?"

"Absolutely," I tossed over my shoulder. I stopped by Beverly's desk and told her I was going out for lunch.

The middle-aged-woman glanced at the clock on her desk. "But's it's not even close to noon."

"This is business," I told her.

Her mouth flattened into a disapproving line as if to say, "Your father never took an early lunch." It might be time for Beverly to retire, I thought as I let Abruzzo escort me to the elevator.

I wasn't a businessman like my father. I hadn't been in the game for years, and I definitely wasn't powerful. I was just his daughter. I had his last name but my own way of doing things. He never wanted me to be anything other than what I was. I really loved that about him.

"Where are we going?" Abruzzo asked once we got into the lobby. I pulled out my leather gloves from my long cashmere coat pockets and slid them on. Boston cold wasn't like New York cold. Boston cold was *wet*. And you felt it in your bones.

"My favorite Irish pub," I said with a grin.

"Ah, you can take the girl out of Ireland…"

"I was born in Ireland," I told him as a doorman pushed open the glass door for me. I thanked him with a nod and smile. He was new and I hadn't yet had time to introduce myself, but he clearly knew me when he said, "Have a good day, Ms. O'Malley."

"I know you were born in Ireland," Abruzzo said.

I shot him a look just as a blast of cold air came around the side of the building, whipping my hair. He grasped my elbow when he saw that I struggled on the ice in my heels.

"Your father told me," he explained. "When we had lunch last year."

"You met with my father last year?" I instinctively moved closer to him, telling myself his warmth was nothing more than a shield from the weather. I wouldn't admit that I enjoyed his touch. It wasn't possessive or aggressive. Strange, because the night I'd met him I wanted to punch him in his perfect smiling mouth.

"We started discussions last year. He was searching for the perfect building for me. He hadn't found it yet, though."

"What kind of business?"

"I'll tell you after you have a full stomach. Italians do not discuss business until after the meal."

"Want to make sure your guest is loosened up from wine and pasta so you can get what you want out of a deal, eh?"

"Something like that. Where is this place? My nose is about to fall off my face."

"Just up ahead." About ten feet later, I turned to a restaurant with a red door. The black awning was accented in gold thread and it hung on fiercely, despite the winter wind trying to blow if off.

Abruzzo got the heavy door for me and I stepped inside. The smells of corned beef and cabbage wafted from the back kitchen.

"Could you be more of a stereotype?" Abruzzo asked with a laugh.

"And where would you have taken me to lunch," I demanded. "An Italian restaurant?"

"There are no good Italian restaurants in Boston."

"Liar."

"It's true. All bastardized versions of Italian food. Trust me. I'll cook for you one night and prove to you I know better."

Before I could say anything about Abruzzo's over familiarity, the door to the kitchen swung open and a tall, thin man barreled his way past the unmanned bar.

"You," he stated.

"Me," I agreed.

He gazed at me with fierce blue eyes, and then a smile widened his craggy face. "Come here, you!"

Chapter Nineteen

"SEAN, I'd like you to meet Mr. Ori Abruzzo," I introduced, pulling back from his hug.

The man my brother was named after held out his hand. Abruzzo took it and pumped it a few times before dropping it.

"What brings you by before we're open?" Sean demanded, a knowing twinkle in his eye.

"I was hoping you could give us two plates of the O'Shaunessy special. And two pints."

"Good thing I like you," Sean muttered like he was annoyed but completely unable to hold in his smile. He dashed back to the kitchen, leaving me alone with Abruzzo.

Without waiting for Abruzzo to say anything, I shrugged out of my coat and walked to the backroom of the pub. It was off the main floor and away from the door.

I gently laid my coat on the booth and then slid into the corner seat.

"Can I have that spot?" Abruzzo asked.

"What's wrong with the seat across from me?"

"I have a quirk," he admitted with a rueful smile. "I don't like my back to the door."

My brows furrowed in thought. My father had been the same way. So had Sasha. To anyone else, Abruzzo's request wouldn't have been given a second thought. But I was the daughter of a corrupt businessman with ties to the IRA. My ex-boyfriend had been the leader of the Russian mob in New York City.

"Who are you?" I demanded quietly so as not to alert Sean.

His dark eyes held my gaze. "A friend."

"This was a mistake," I said, climbing out of the seat and reaching for my coat.

"Please." Abruzzo's hand on mine stopped me. "Please let me explain."

I looked at our hands and then up at him. "Okay. I'm listening." I tried to calm the racing of my heart, praying Ori Abruzzo couldn't hear it.

Abruzzo looked over his shoulder to the closed door of the kitchen and then glanced back at me. "You trust him?"

I nodded. I wasn't about to tell Abruzzo this was the place where my father had put together all his under-the-table deals. Sean had fed some of the most notorious mobsters in Boston. But he was Irish, through and through, and his loyalty to my father had never been questioned. Therefore I never questioned it. I also knew there was a loaded shotgun behind the bar.

The life of white-collar criminals didn't scare me. The unknown did.

I stood up and moved away so that Abruzzo could take the seat in the corner so his back was against the wall. He let out an obvious sigh. Sinking down into the chair across from him, I folded my hands in my lap and waited. So did Abruzzo.

The swinging door banged open, hitting the wall, and a moment later, Sean placed two plates of food in front of us.

I looked up at him and smiled. "Thank you."

"Give me just a second to grab the pints." The restaurant phone rang, pulling his attention.

"I got the pints," I said, moving to get up.

Sean sent me a grateful look and then dashed to answer the phone. I got up from the chair, my eyes on Abruzzo. He waited patiently, his face giving away nothing.

I went behind the bar and poured two pints of Guinness, letting them stop half-way. They needed to settle for a few minutes. Sean was yelling at someone on the other end of the phone, and then he hung up.

"Fucking meat guy screwed me. I gotta run out."

I swallowed, not wanting to be alone with Abruzzo in the bar. I felt like the biggest idiot. I'd let my guard down.

Sean grabbed his coat and left, the sound of the door shutting completely ominous.

"Are you coming back to the table?" Abruzzo called, amusement in his tone.

"Just waiting for the Guinness to settle," I called back.

"I guess now is not the time to tell you that I hate Guinness?"

For some reason, his statement made me smile. And I rationalized that a man who could tease and flirt over lunch after admitting he wasn't what he seemed wasn't going to hurt me. It was perhaps, the stupidest thing I'd thought lately. Then again, there was that shotgun underneath the bar. Just in case. And it was within my reach.

"Bring the plates to the bar," I called to him.

"You want to sit right in front of the door in case you need to make a break for it? When my charm becomes too much?"

I laughed. "Yeah. Exactly."

"I'll humor you," Abruzzo said. He picked up the plates and came toward me. I grabbed napkins and spare silverware from the end of the bar and set them down.

"Are you going to sit next to me?" Abruzzo asked.

"Nope. I'll eat standing up. Thanks." I pulled one plate in front of me but didn't make a move to take a bite. "Okay. So who the hell are you?"

Abruzzo maneuvered himself up onto a bar chair. "I am who I said I am. My name is Ori Abruzzo, and your father and I were discussing a business venture."

"Go on."

"I was going to open an Italian restaurant in my name and your father"—he cleared his throat—"was going to launder money."

Most daughters would flinch when they heard about their deceased father's illegal dealings. Balk, maybe.

Laundering money with Ori Abruzzo was my father's plan. It wasn't going to be mine.

"Mr. Abruzzo," I began.

"Ori. Call me Ori."

"Ori," I repeated with a nod. "I have no issue with the agreement you and my father discussed. In fact, if he were still alive, it would still be a part of the plan. But I've taken over the family business—and I'll be honest, I have no idea what I'm doing." I leaned over the bar. "I know even less about the other types of businesses my father was involved in."

Nor did I have any desire to go down that road, I didn't say. I wouldn't know the first thing about it. And besides, I was a woman who'd stood on the sidelines while her man engaged in nefarious activities; I didn't run them.

"I think you're doing better than you give yourself credit for," Ori stated.

I shrugged. "Neither here nor there. It's my father's legacy. I can't knowingly flush it down the toilet. Now if it happens because of my inability and stupidity, that's another story."

"You're quite capable, Quinn."

It was the first time he'd said my name, and I was surprised to find that I liked it.

No. I didn't like it. This was Ori Abruzzo. I had to remember that he'd called me a rich girl cock tease, and only now he was saying what he thought I wanted to hear so we'd get into business together.

"You don't know me," I told him, finally picking up my fork so I could take a bite of one of my favorite dishes.

"No," he agreed. "I don't. Only from what your father chose to share with me. But, I'd like to remedy that."

"Remedy what?" I set my fork down and picked up my pint—*when did I become the lunchtime drinker*—and took a sip.

"Getting to know you. I think I'd like to get to know you." Ori's eyes were dark and focused on me like a laser.

"I just got out of something," I blurted out.

He nodded. "I gathered."

"Did you?"

"You seem…nervous."

"Cautious," I clarified. "You're not one of those guys are you?"

"One of those guys?" he asked in amusement.

"You don't expect me to date you now that we have no business relationship."

"Quinn O'Malley, you're blunt."

"No point beating around the bush, wouldn't you agree?"

"I do."

"I don't want to go into business with you."

"Yeah, you made that clear," he said, dry amusement in his tone. "But who said I wanted to date you?"

"Well, you did. The night of the gala."

"Ah, no." He rubbed his jaw. "I was thinking about something else entirely."

I rolled my eyes. "Fine. I know what you wanted—I'm not giving you that either."

"So no business relationship, no dating, and no—"

"*Definitely* not that."

Ori smiled. "Okay. Whatever you want." He took a bite of his food. "This is really good."

I blinked, surprised he'd taken my rejection so easily. I wasn't sure I wanted him to give up that quickly.

"Quinn, let me give you a piece of advice. If you want to play poker with the big boys, learn how to bluff. Your face shows everything you're thinking."

Chapter Twenty

"You headed back to your office?" Ori asked.

I nodded. Even though all I wanted to do was take a nap, I had to go back. If I didn't go back, Beverly would no doubt notice and comment on it the next morning. I couldn't let Beverly's judgmental attitude affect me. She wasn't the boss. I was the boss. I needed to act like it. If I wanted to have a martini lunch, then I would. And it hadn't been a martini—it had only been half a Guinness. Maybe I was exhausted from all the verbal sparring.

"I'll walk you," Ori said.

"Really trying to prove you're not the asshole from the gala, huh?"

"Is it working?" He took my elbow as we stepped outside.

"Hmm. Sure." Truth was, he was rapidly changing how I viewed him. Despite being a criminal, I didn't judge him on that. It would've been hypocritical, considering my father's affiliations. And Sasha's.

A pang of regret went through me when I thought of

him. I didn't think I could go back to the office. Pieces of me were shaking loose. Jagged edges lanced my heart.

"You know what?" I said, turning to the street. "I'm gonna catch a cab."

"But the office—"

"I'm going home. Thanks for lunch."

"You treated, remember?" he said with a rueful smile.

I needed to get out of there. It had started to snow while we'd been having lunch. If I'd been with Sasha, I would've turned my face up to the sky and opened my mouth, wanting to catch the white flakes on my tongue. I'd let them dissolve, turn my mouth cold. And then I'd kiss him, and I would've been warm.

The picture was so real I didn't move when a cab drove up to the curb and stopped. It wasn't until Ori was opening the cab door and waiting for me to get in that I realized I'd stopped moving, frozen.

"Thank you," I murmured.

He smiled but didn't say anything as I climbed into the car. He shut the door and then stood there until I gave the driver my address. The cab drove away, and Ori became a speck in the distance.

I focused on breathing in and out.

It would've been easier if Sasha had died. If he'd died, I could have mourned him, mourned us. But as long as he lived, there was an ember of hope. And even him leaving me hadn't doused the flame.

I'd never been in love before Sasha. Sure, I'd thought I'd found it. With a few guys from college, but I'd always questioned it. But with Sasha I just *knew*.

Love was only the beginning, and it didn't mean a relationship was going to be easy. I'd had to reconcile Sasha's love for Barrett. A lot of the time I'd felt like I was second best, that he'd settled for me. But then he showed me the cigarette burns on his skin and told me of his childhood.

He'd never told Barrett about his childhood.

I'd been disgusted with myself for feeling like I'd one-upped her. Like I'd earned his secrets. For some reason, when he confided in me, it felt like an achievement, a victory. He'd let me in—in a way he never let Barrett in.

It meant something to me.

Lost in thought, I didn't realize the cab had stopped in front of my house. I quickly swiped my card and then embarked out into the bitter cold. I unlocked the door and breathed in the quiet. Setting my keys down on the foyer table, I kicked off my heels.

I ran a hand across the back of my neck and shivered. Ever since I'd cut my hair, I'd noticed a dramatic shift in my body temperature. I was cold all the time now. I had no protection against the elements. Leaving my coat on, I walked into the sitting room and sat down on the couch. The afternoon sunlight—what little of it existed—had already started to disappear, leaving the room mostly in shadows.

I pulled my phone out of my coat pocket. Unlocking the screen, I then navigated to a password-encrypted file. After I typed the passcode, the photograph came into focus.

It had been taken four months after Sasha had left. There shouldn't have been a spark of light in my eyes. I should've looked shuddered, unhappy. My gaze landed on the slight swell of my belly. It was hardly discernible—you really had to look.

I closed my phone and set it aside and thought about the general theme of my life. The men I loved left me. Sickness, selfishness, the inability to cope. I never thought of myself as the strong one, but it turned out I was the only one who was actually reliable.

The next morning, I walked into O'Malley Properties and was greeted by Beverly's disapproving gaze. Apparently, I didn't warrant the same level of respect that my father had once commanded.

"Delivery for you. It's on your desk," she said and then went back to eating her breakfast sandwich.

"Thank you." I strolled through the door to my office and stopped. On the desk was a bouquet of white orchids. I slowly shut the door, and then my feet ate up space as I went to the flowers. A white card with silver script peered at me from the blooms. I reached for it, knowing whom it was from before I even opened it.

The handwriting was scrolled and perfect—clearly not a man's handwriting, but I looked at the signature. It was an ineligible scrawl. The message was a taunt, a throwing down of the gauntlet. Ori Abruzzo was trying to engage me into a verbal sparring match.

Why did men like such a challenge?

It had been the same with Sasha. I thought of the night we'd met. I'd been having dinner with Shannon in Boston. Sasha had sauntered in, commanding the air around him. His eyes had locked on mine, and he'd immediately approached our table. I'd dismissed him, even though all I wanted to do was head to the bar and share a bottle of wine, learn everything I could about the enigmatic man who walked with the stride of a predator. But I wasn't the type of woman who ditched a friend for a man.

When dessert had arrived, sent from Sasha himself, his number was written on the plate in chocolate sauce.

"You have to call him," Shannon had said.

"We'll see," I'd replied, all the while committing to memory the phone number. He hadn't even told me his name. All I had was the phone number. I waited a week before reaching out and the only reason I did was because I couldn't get him out of my mind. When we'd locked eyes in the restaurant, I'd felt something inside of me jar loose.

I'd called. He'd answered. And then he'd flown me to Manhattan for dinner, and I'd never left.

Shaking my head, I dispelled the memory of our early courtship. Ori Abruzzo wasn't Sasha, but I recognized the same steely determination in his persona. Powerful men with a drive to succeed would stop at nothing. The question? Was I intrigued enough to go out to dinner with a man who wasn't the love of my life?

Chapter Twenty-One

"THIS IS A TERRIBLE IDEA," I said to Shannon as I popped my head out of the walk-in closet.

Shannon perched on my bed, looking like a fragile wren. Her cream fisherman's sweater hung on her frame, and I knew she'd borrowed it from Patrick. "Why is this a terrible idea?" she asked. Without any shame, she unbuttoned the top snap of her jeans and let out a sigh of relief.

"I need new pants," she muttered.

"This is a terrible idea because I haven't been on a date in three years." I held up a black dress.

Shannon made a face. "Maybe a dress that doesn't make you look like you're in mourning."

"I *am* in mourning," I snapped.

She sighed. "You didn't date Sasha. You were just....together. Dating is good for you."

"Says the girl who married her high school sweetheart and hasn't slept with anyone else." My shoulders slumped. "Sorry. That was mean."

"Yeah, it was," Shannon chirped with a smile. "But Patrick is really good in bed."

"How would you know? You have nothing to compare him to."

"There's something to be said with only having been with one person. We've grown and changed together."

"That's great. Seriously. No sarcasm meant." I sighed. My wardrobe was downright depressing. When I'd moved back to Boston, my clothes had evolved from bright jewel tones to grays and blacks.

I flipped through the hangers until I got to the back and discovered a long-forgotten dress. A ruby red confection that concealed my chest but showed off my entire back. With my newly bobbed hair, it would be perfect. If I still fit into it. I'd lost weight.

I slid into the dress and looked at myself in the full-length mirror. It didn't hang off me, which was good. But Shannon would deliver the final verdict.

"Okay, what about this?" I asked, coming out.

Shannon's eyes widened.

"Wait for it," I said and then turned.

"Yes. Absolutely yes. That's perfect!"

"Great." I moved to take the dress off and then thought better of it and sat on the bed next to Shannon. "What the hell am I doing?"

Shannon grasped my hand and held it tight. "You're living, Quinn. There's nothing wrong with that."

"It's strange…how fast life can change."

"So take dating slow. Very slow."

I shot her an amused look. "When have I ever taken anything slow? I'm an all or nothing kind of girl."

"Normally, yeah. The old Quinn is definitely that type of girl. But you're a woman now. And you've lived through a lot of tragedies. Tragedies change you."

Shaking my head, I let go of her hand and stood. "I

miss her sometimes. The old Quinn. She was brash and carefree. She was the life of the party."

"She's still the life of the party."

I looked at her. "Maybe." My eyes dipped to her stomach, and I bit my lip.

"What is it?" she asked.

"Nothing," I said, shaking off the somber direction of my thoughts. "Just"—I shrugged—"life doesn't always work out how you plan."

"Your life isn't over," she said quietly. "Why do you talk about it like it is?"

I looked up at the ceiling so the unbidden tears wouldn't spill down my cheeks. "I don't think I want that life. Not with someone else." I glanced at her. "Don't you see, Shannon? Anyone else is second place."

Color faded from Shannon's cheeks, and she nodded carefully. I knew she wanted to say something, but lately, she'd been holding her tongue, like she didn't want to set me off.

"Maybe one day, I'll feel differently," I mused. "Maybe with enough passage of time, I won't want to cry into my pillow every night."

"You cry into your pillow every night?"

I snorted. "No. I won't let myself."

"You should. You keep it all bottled up, Quinn. Maybe it needs to come out—really come out. So you can grieve and move on. Not keep picking at this—this *wound*."

I lifted the dress over my head and carefully laid it on the bed, not caring I was in a pair of panties and no bra. Shannon and I had grown up together. There was nothing to hide from her. Not even the slight silver lines on my lower belly. There was no amount of aloe or cocoa butter that would get rid of them.

She'd stayed with me. In the hospital. After.

"Dimitri visited me last week." I pulled on a pair of leggings and a long-sleeved shirt.

Shannon unfolded herself from my bed, and we headed downstairs to the sitting room. "What did he want? Did Sasha…"

I crouched down to turn on the fireplace. "No. It wasn't on Sasha's orders. Dimitri said he hasn't heard from Sasha in months. Sasha signed *Krasnyy* over to me."

"Whoa."

"Yeah."

"Fucker," Shannon seethed, her cheeks heating. She rarely cursed.

"Fucker, indeed," I agreed. "So tell me what that means because I sure as hell don't know. He leaves me a note that tells me he's not the man he used to be, to mourn him, and love another."

"So *Legends of the Fall*, by the way," she interjected.

I smiled at the brief moment of levity. "Seriously. But then he gives me his bar. Gives it to me. He couldn't give it to Barrett?"

"Okay, devil's advocate. If he'd given it to Barrett, wouldn't you have been pissed?" Shannon knew all about my strange relationship with Barrett Campbell—she knew about Sasha's relationship with her too.

"I don't know," I admitted. I finally stood from my crouch, my legs tingling. "Part of me would've been pissed, for sure. The other part would've been grateful."

Shannon pulled up her legs to her chest and rested her chin on her knees. "So what are you going to do with *Krasnyy?*"

"Sell it maybe. I don't know. I know just as much about owning a club as I do about real estate."

"He really is a bastard. For putting you in that position.

Do you think… Do you really think he's not keeping tabs on you?"

"I don't know."

"Do you want him to be keeping tabs on you?"

Shaking my head, I sent her a wry smile. "And thus continues this endless cycle."

Shannon was quiet for a moment, and then she said, "Wear the red dress when you go out with Ori Abruzzo. And leave your heels on when you fuck him."

"My, my, you're the crass one tonight."

She tossed long blonde hair over her shoulder. "Maybe this is the new Shannon."

Chapter Twenty-Two

Shannon went home and two hours before I was supposed to meet Ori for dinner, I chickened out. I called him, praying it went to voicemail so I could blow him off without having to talk to him.

"Hello, Quinn."

No dice.

"Uhm. Ori. Hi." I paused, unsure of how to go on.

"Did you call me for something?" he asked. I could hear the amusement in his tone.

"Yes. Yes, I did." I took a deep breath. "I have to cancel tonight. I'm really sorry."

"Ah," he said.

I could picture his face wreathed in a smile, leaning back in an office chair as he played with a pen. I didn't even know if he had an office, but he struck me as the type of man who sat at a desk, fiddled with pens, and made comments like "ah" when a woman was ditching him last minute.

"Yeah, so I'm really sorry. I'll call and reschedule." I quickly hung up and then pressed my cell phone to my forehead. "He's an idiot if he believes my excuse," I said to no one.

I tried to push away the feelings of guilt. I wasn't ready to date. I might not ever be ready to date. And despite the fact that Ori's first impression had left a lot to be desired, he'd grown on me. He was interesting to talk to and—shocker of all shockers—I liked the back and forth.

It was just past sunset when I opened a bottle of red. As I took my wine to the den, there was a knock on the front door.

Frowning, I went to the door and looked through the peephole. Ori Abruzzo was standing outside, coat collar flipped up to protect him from the weather, carrying paper grocery bags in each hand.

I unlocked the door and opened it. "What are you doing here?"

He smiled. "Can I come in? It's cold out."

"Sure," I said, drawing out the word as I stepped back. He came into the foyer, and I closed the door.

"You chickened out," he stated.

"What? No," I brazened. "I didn't chicken out. Something came up."

"Oh yeah? What came up, exactly?"

I blinked and then feigned a cough. "I'm sick."

His amused gazed traveled to my wine glass. "A hot toddy is better than wine for that."

My shoulders slumped. "I chickened out."

"Why?"

How did I tell him without *telling him* because there wasn't an elevator pitch for my life. "I—because."

Ori stared at me for a long moment and then asked, "What kind of wine are you drinking?"

"Pinot from Napa."

"Stop immediately," he commanded. "Don't go any further. Where's the kitchen?"

In bemusement, I pointed. Ori sauntered down the hallway toward the kitchen. I followed at a slower pace. He'd set the grocery bags onto the counter and was now pulling out ingredients.

"What is all this?" I asked. I picked up a head of garlic and sniffed it. It was so potent it nearly made my eyes water.

"Dinner. Or it will be." He shrugged out of his coat and hung it on the back of a kitchen chair.

"Why are you here?"

"Wine opener?" he asked.

I pulled out the corkscrew and handed it to him. He deftly opened a bottle he'd brought with him in three movements. "A baby Amarone. From Italy," he said with a roguish grin. "I need glasses."

Setting aside my wine, I then went to retrieve two clean glasses. Crystal. Ori poured and then handed one to me.

"Why are you here?" I asked again.

"Take a sip and then I'll tell you."

Rolling my eyes, I lifted the glass to my nose. I sniffed and my mouth instantly watered. I took a small sip, let it linger on my tongue, and then swallowed.

"Wow," was all I could say.

He grinned, obviously pleased. Ori pushed up the sleeves of his gray sweater, and I finally noticed what he was wearing. A pair of black slacks. Dressed down. Way down.

"Why am I here?" he asked. "Well, I realized that asking you out to dinner was maybe a little too fast for you." He looked at me. "You remind me of a scared little fawn. *Cerbiatto.*"

I ignored the Italian word, because it sounded too

much like an endearment, and moved along. "And you thought barging into my house with," I glanced at the counter, "ingredients—"

"And wine," he added.

"—Wasn't too fast?"

"Okay, you sit." He pointed to one of the stools nestled under the island. "And we're both going to pretend you're not all broken and defeated."

"What did you just say to me?" I snapped.

He pushed my glass of wine toward me. "Drink. Trust me."

Silently grumbling, I took a sip and then took a seat. "I'm not broken and defeated."

"Okay."

"I'm *not.*"

"Then why did you cancel last minute?"

I closed my mouth and refused to answer.

"Uh huh. Thought so." He went to the sink and washed his hands.

"So, what are you cooking?" I asked, reluctantly intrigued by all the ingredients on the counter. I was always amazed by the people who knew their way around the kitchen. My mother had been a good cook. Must've skipped a generation.

"Spaghetti Carbonara," he said. "If I had the time, I would've made the pasta by hand. So"—he picked up the package of high-end spaghetti—"this will have to do."

"Are you going to ask me to help?"

He smiled. "Do you want to help?"

"No." I grinned. "I'm good here, watching the show."

Ori chuckled. "All right, but you have to entertain me if I cook for you."

He was a whiz in a kitchen, and he moved with efficiency. He chopped onions, grated cheese, all the while waiting for the water to boil.

"Why a restaurant?" I asked him. "For a business with my father, why a restaurant?"

He dumped diced pancetta into a sizzling pan. "It's familiar to me. I used to work as a cook in my mother's restaurant."

"Really?" I asked.

Ori nodded. "When I was in my twenties."

"Does your mother still have the restaurant?"

"She does. Though, she's not as active as she used to be." He paused as if he wanted to say more but wasn't as sure.

"Why not?" I pushed.

"After my brother's death, some of the spark went out of her. The restaurant was her place, but even that didn't offer her the comfort of losing her oldest son."

"Awful," I murmured. "A mother losing her child. Were you close to your brother?"

Ori kept his eyes on the pan as he stirred the pancetta. "No. Not really." He sighed. "He was"—he paused and looked at me—"such an ass. But he was my brother."

Chapter Twenty-Three

I RAISED MY GLASS. "To asshole brothers."

Ori raised his and smiled softly. "To asshole brothers."

"My brother is currently in London," I said, setting my glass aside.

"Doing what?"

"Gallivanting, I guess." I shook my head. "He cut out pretty much as soon as Dad got his diagnosis. Sean doesn't really do well with emotion."

"So your brother left you here to deal with your dad's illness—and death—all on your own?"

"Yeah."

"What about your stepmother?"

I cocked my head to the side. "You really do know a lot about my family."

"Gotta know the people you want to go into business with."

"That's true."

"Besides, I had dinner with your father and his wife."

"Jessica," I sneered. "She left the wake early. She's

somewhere in Vermont, working through her grief at one of those spas."

"Ah. So you really are the glue. No wonder your father left you his business."

"You know, I'm not really liking the tone of this first date. First dates are supposed to be fun and flirty. Not dark and heavy."

"I thought you didn't want to date me. This is just two friends hanging out getting to know each other."

"But you brought wine. And food to cook."

"You don't drink with friends? Your friends don't cook for you?"

"No, they do, but my friends don't ask me to go away with them to Bermuda on a first encounter."

He tossed me a charming smile over his shoulder. "I can be fun and flirty—but only if you want this to be an actual date."

"Prove it."

"Ask me questions."

"What like, favorite ice cream? Favorite color? Those sorts of questions?"

"Mint chocolate chip and orange. But for the record, those are boring questions."

"How old were you when you lost your virginity?" I fired back.

"Seventeen. And before you ask, it was with my sister's friend from college who was nineteen."

"*C'est scandal!*" I mocked.

He chuckled. "Now you."

"Ah, let's see. I was fifteen and it was the captain of the football team. He was a senior."

"Of course he was. Please tell me he didn't take your virginity and then ignore you the next day."

I snorted. "No. In fact, he asked me to be his girlfriend,

and I turned him down. I became the most popular girl in school overnight." Thus starting my evolution into professional party girl.

"Why did you turn him down?" he wondered. He looked at the timer and set it and then threw the spaghetti into the boiling pot of water.

"Because he was no good in bed," I stated matter of fact.

Ori laughed. "Yeah, sounds about right. What high school senior jock is good in bed?"

"Now *this* is a first date," I said with a smile.

"Next question."

"Food allergies?"

"None."

"Same. What's the worst lie you ever told?"

"Let me see." He stirred the noodles to make sure they didn't stick. He cracked eggs into a mixing bowl and then whisked in cream. "I can't think of a lie."

"And Washington didn't chop down the cherry tree," I teased.

"I'm sure I've lied. I just can't remember one at the moment. Pick another question."

"Biggest failure?"

"Not being able to get you to go to Bermuda with me."

I laughed, which is exactly what Ori intended.

"So maybe you can answer some of my questions." The timer beeped and Ori strained the noodles. And then he was like an octopus, his hands everywhere at once, plating the food. It had been a long time since someone had used the kitchen with such thought. The aromas were tantalizing, homey.

"Your mom taught you how to cook, didn't she?" I asked as Ori set a plate in front of me. I leaned over and closed my eyes. When I opened my eyes, I saw that Ori was watching me with a predatory stillness.

He smiled slowly. "Yes. She taught me."

I twirled the spaghetti onto the fork and waited for it to cool just a bit before tasting it. Salt, pork, and cheese mixed together to make a delicious experience.

Sasha had never cooked for me. It had never bothered me. But here was a man who brought his passion to the plate. And it was heady.

"This is incredible."

"I know," he said, smug arrogance radiating off him. He served himself, but instead of moving to another stool, he remained standing at the island. Purposefully casual, which I appreciated.

"First memory of you cooking," I said, ignoring his boastful praise of himself.

"Fileting *branzini* for the evening special. I was six."

"Wielding a knife at six, huh?"

He shrugged. "What's your earliest memory of cooking?"

I thought for a moment and took a sip of wine. "Ah. Christmas cookies. With my grandmother. I think I was four."

"Were you covered in sugar and spice?" he teased.

"And everything nice." I shook my head. "Yeah, I think I got flour and sugar everywhere. Made the cookies taste better. I can to this day, remember the smell and taste of those sugar cookies. Is that weird?"

"Not even a little bit. Certain memories are so powerful. Smells too. Whenever I get a first whiff of chopped up raw garlic, I think about family dinners with aunts and uncles, all my cousins. Escarole with garlic and olive oil." He sighed. "Pretty much a staple of every Italian family dinner."

I thought about some of the other smells that triggered memories. Lavender—my mother's favorite scent, and the one my father had burning by his bedside while he was in hospice. It still hadn't been able to cover the underlying, putrid smell of decay.

Lavender had once been a fragrance of comfort. Now, it reminded me of death.

Wood smoke and the metallic smell of blood. Reminding me of Sasha's burnt body. His flesh warped from flames.

Ori and I fell silent, and we didn't speak until we'd cleared our plates. "That was delicious," I said. "But you already know that."

"I do."

He picked up the plates and set them in the sink.

"Don't even think about doing the dishes," I stated.

"I wouldn't dream of it." He winked. "Does that mean you're doing the dishes?"

"Absolutely not. Mrs. Robbins will do them in the morning."

"And she would be?"

"The housekeeper."

"Does she do your laundry, too?" he quipped.

"She does." I wasn't embarrassed that I didn't do household chores myself. Call me spoiled, but it was how I'd grown up.

"What about when you went to college? Did you have someone take care of you then, too?"

"Are you judging me?"

"No. I'm just curious." He tilted his head to one side and then reached for the bottle of wine. He topped off our glasses before setting it down.

"Let's go into the sitting room," I stated. "It's cold enough to turn on the fireplace." I picked up my glass of wine and walked out of the kitchen. "Besides, I'd rather be comfortable while you interrogate me."

"No interrogation," he promised. "Just avid curiosity."

I flipped on the main light and then quickly dimmed it. Ori took a seat in one of the comfortable chairs, and I squatted to turn on the fireplace. The flames flared to life and even before the fan started to blow, I shivered from the warmth.

"Why are you curious about me?" I asked, taking a seat on the couch across from him.

"It's not often you meet people you want to know better. Do you know what I mean? Everyone is just so…"

"Dull?"

"Yeah. Dull." He laughed and looked at me, his gaze steady, like he was trying to figure me out. "You're anything but dull."

Chapter Twenty-Four

THE GRANDFATHER CLOCK in the hallway chimed. Ori looked at his watch to confirm the time. "It's eleven."

"Already?" I asked. The night had flown by.

"Careful, that sounds like you actually enjoyed my company," he teased, setting his empty wine glass onto a coaster.

"I did enjoy your company," I said, surprising us both.

"Think we can do it again?" He moved toward the hallway and then walked back into the kitchen to grab his coat. He shrugged into it as he waited for my answer.

"We can do it again."

"Maybe in public next time?"

"I'll think about it," I said.

"It's okay, my little *Cerbiatto*. I'll tread softly."

"Please don't call me that."

He looked at me and zipped up his coat. "You don't like endearments?"

"No, I don't." I crossed my arms over my chest and pinned him with a stare. Endearments were for familiarity, for parents and children, for lovers. Ori and I had spent a few hours together, but we didn't know each other, not in the way you knew someone's soul. I still wasn't sure I wanted to know someone like that ever again. Losing it once had almost destroyed me.

"Do you keep everyone at arms length?" he demanded.

"Yes. And you would too if you—" I cut myself off. I didn't want to explain, and I certainly didn't want him to feel sorry for me. Sometimes I pitied my current outcome, and then I'd get angry with myself. I'd lost people, I'd lost love. But I was still standing on the battlefield. I was still holding my weapons.

"If?" Ori prodded.

I shook my head. "I'm not doing this."

"What? Explaining yourself? What do you gain if you don't share with me what you've lived through?"

"What will I lose if I'm vulnerable?" I shot back. "If I've learned anything, it's that you can't rely on anyone but yourself. Parents get sick and die. Brothers leave."

I didn't bother mentioning Sasha. His betrayal was the hardest of all. At the end of the day, I didn't blame my father for dying. And Sean's leaving pissed me off, but that was classic Sean. Sasha slinking off into the night, never to be heard from again, didn't make an ounce of sense to me. I never would've left him.

Never.

But I'd been easy to leave, apparently.

"We're not all the same, Quinn," Ori said softly, dark eyes on mine.

"It's not enough to say it," I whispered. "I can't—He was never supposed to leave me. You don't leave the ones you love."

You didn't leave the woman you rescued from a burning boat. You didn't rush into the flames, with no thought to yourself to save her life. You didn't walk out on her when she was there every step of the way.

"Quinn—"

"You should go," I said, putting my hand on his arm and urging him to the door. I opened it and waited. Cold air hit me in the face and brushed my neck. I shivered while Ori Abruzzo stared at me, no desire to leave.

"You should let yourself be happy," he told me.

"I have been happy. It never lasts."

"I'd like to kill the guy that broke your heart."

"Hearts mend, Ori. It's my faith in humanity that needs restoring."

He looked at me one last time and then said, "Good night, Quinn."

I shut the door after him and then leaned against it. The house suddenly felt empty. I walked back into the kitchen and looked at the dirty dishes—a reminder of the meal we'd shared, when for just a moment, I hadn't felt so alone.

Damn Ori, for making me want to share my past. It was better for me to stay aloof. I wouldn't get hurt that way. I'd had enough hurt, and sharing it wouldn't make me feel better. It wouldn't change the outcome.

Leaving the mess in the kitchen, I went back to the sitting room. I poured myself a glass of vodka and sat by the fire, contemplating how to move forward.

I wanted nothing to do with *Krasnyy*. I didn't even want to be the absent owner. Why had Sasha given it to me?

It was midnight and I thought about calling Shannon, but she was pregnant, no doubt asleep, and curled up with Patrick. And she wasn't the person I wanted to talk to.

Before I could consider it, I pressed a button. The line rang a few times, and then a husky voice answered.

"Sorry I woke you," I said, taking a sip of vodka.

"You don't sound sorry," Barrett said. "Is everything okay?"

"Nothing emergent."

"You just fancied a chat at…midnight Boston time? You do know it's five AM here, and I've got three boys who will wake me up in about an hour. So your crisis better be really good."

"Not a crisis," I assured her. "But I needed someone to talk to."

"About Sasha?" she guessed.

"Yeah."

I heard the muffled sounds of Flynn saying something to her, but then Barrett came back on the line. "Give me a second to get downstairs."

I stared into the glass of vodka—*I hadn't been a vodka drinker until him*—as I waited for Barrett to find a private, quiet place. The Campbells lived in a restored castle in Dornoch, Scotland, so finding a quiet place wouldn't be difficult.

I sipped from the glass of vodka. Cheap vodka, all you felt was the burn, but with high-end stuff, there were actual flavors. An acquired taste.

Barrett sighed. "All right. I'm in the library. What's on your mind?"

"He left me *Krasnyy*. Did you know that?"

"No," she said, surprise coloring her tone. "I had no idea."

"I don't want it. What do I do?"

"Do? Do you have to *do* anything?"

"Dimitri paid me a visit. He wanted—hell—I don't know what he wanted. He said it was time for another ad campaign and that I should model for it. But I can't do it, Barrett. My life is here. The club is in New York. And it's Sasha's place. It's not mine."

"You don't want it." Her tone wasn't at all accusatory, just matter of fact.

"No, I don't want it. So what do I do?"

"Sell it."

My breath hitched. It was one thing for me to say it. It was another for Barrett to suggest it.

"Guess you don't really want to sell it, huh?"

"I should just gift it to Dimitri."

I didn't ask Barrett if she thought Sasha was ever coming back, but maybe leaving *Krasnyy* in the Russian family wasn't such a bad idea.

"It's not like you need the money," Barrett said with a small laugh.

"Right?" I shook my head even though she couldn't see it. I never wanted for things or comfort. I hadn't grown up like Sasha who'd earned everything. He'd taken more than his fair share, but you didn't stay the leader of the Russian mafia without throwing your weight around. Though I guessed Dimitri was now considered the king, since Sasha had disappeared and given up his claim.

"What's really going on, Quinn? I know you didn't call to ask about *Krasnyy.* You knew what you were going to do anyway. So what is it?"

I pressed my fingers to my forehead and rubbed. "I don't—dating. I want to know about dating."

"I'm not sure I understand the question. Are you thinking about dating?" She paused. "Or have you met someone?"

Chapter Twenty-Five

"No, I haven't met someone," I lied.

"You know it would be okay if you did," Barrett said gently.

"I'm not looking for your permission."

"No? Then why did you call me at midnight?"

I paused, my fingers wrapped around the nearly empty glass. The flames danced behind the crystal, and I was momentarily entranced by it. "It feels disloyal," I admitted.

"Then maybe you're not ready."

"But what if I want to be ready? What if—What if there's someone who makes me want to be ready, but I'm just not—I can't quite—Fuck. I've had too much wine."

"You think too much," she said with amusement. "Dating doesn't have to mean anything. It just means you're open to possibilities. Don't you want to be open, Quinn? Don't you want"—she swallowed—"a partner? Children?"

"You didn't want children," I reminded her.

"We're not talking about me."

I'd wanted children. Sasha's children. His and no others.

"Maybe I just need to get laid," I said and slugged back the rest of the vodka.

Barrett laughed. "No shame in that."

"Oh, Barrett, what the fuck am I doing? I had a date tonight, and he was…kind of great."

"Really? That's wonderful."

She sounded sincere, like she really wanted me to be happy—even if it wasn't with Sasha.

"You've punished yourself long enough, don't you think?" she asked. Her tone was quiet, prodding. "You've been through a lot, Quinn. Be happy. It's time."

"Just as simple as all that, huh?"

"If you don't like this guy, then don't date him. But if you think there's a chance for you to really be happy, then you should be happy. And happiness with someone else can look different, you know."

"Thanks."

"Can I go back to bed now?"

I laughed. "Yeah. Go back to bed. And Barrett? Thanks."

"Anytime."

We hung up. I sat for a moment and then finally stood. After turning off the fireplace, I headed upstairs to my empty bed.

The next morning, I woke up to the sound of the front door opening followed by my stepmother's voice. I sluggishly pulled myself out of bed and padded my way downstairs. Jessica Bradford O'Malley stood in the foyer hallway as half a dozen people filed into my home.

Jessica saw me coming down the stairs, and she lowered her dark "Jackie O" sunglasses and looked at me. She was a gorgeous woman, with honey blonde hair and blue eyes. I knew what my father saw in her—a blind man could've seen that. But she'd made my father happy despite the fact that I found her…lacking.

"Quinn!" she greeted with a bright smile.

Whatever mood elevators they'd prescribed to her at the "spa" were clearly working their magic. "Hi, Jessica." I blinked the sleep from my eyes, my brain not working. I pulled my sweater tighter around my body. "What's going on?"

Jessica said something to one of the women whose phone was out and she was busy typing away. She didn't even look up when Jessica whispered, merely just nodded her head.

"I'm redecorating," Jessica said.

"Why?"

"Because everything in this house is just so"—Jessica looked around and shuddered—"old."

"Antique," I corrected, suddenly fully awake. I didn't even need a cup of coffee to realize what was going on. My father's lawyer must've gotten ahold of Jessica to let her know what she'd gotten from my father's death.

"Darling," she trilled, "we must find a way to deal with Michael's passing."

"And you think the way to grieve is to get rid of everything that once meant something to my father?"

And to me.

"I was never a fan of the décor," she admitted. "But I didn't protest or demand Michael change anything, because he liked it the way he liked it. But now…"

Jessica started ordering around the six people who were

witnessing our family exchange. She commanded them to go from room to room, cataloguing everything.

I gripped the wooden bannister. "You do realize this is my childhood home."

"Of course, darling. You have the right of first refusal. And you can stay here as long as you like."

Without another word, I turned back around and marched up the stairs. Closing the door to the guest room, I took a deep breath. And then I rushed to the bedside table and grabbed my cell. I had a missed text from Shannon and a call from Ori, but I ignored them both. I thought about calling Dave Flannigan, but what was the point? Jessica owned the house and everything in it. She wasn't being hostile or unreasonable. She was just moving on.

Though Jessica wasn't kicking me out, I didn't want to stay in the house under her decoration. My father was gone. Sean hadn't lived here in years. What was left for me here except a pile of memories?

I closed my eyes and wondered if I could go back to bed. Was there ever going to be a time in my life that wasn't me just having to react to situations being thrown in front of me?

I heard the commotion downstairs. My safe haven wasn't even my haven anymore. I needed to move out of the house—get my own place. Decorate how *I* wanted. I wasn't even sure I knew my own style.

"Quinn!" Jessica called. "Come down here!"

I threw on a pair of jeans and then headed into the bathroom to brush my teeth and wash my face. This wasn't how I envisioned spending my Saturday—readjusting to Jessica's intrusion on my life. We'd coexisted while my father was alive, but she'd had no children with him, so I had no half-siblings. When I left this house, I didn't anticipate weekly family dinners, catching up with Jessica and her life.

Instead of feeling depressed and sad over yet another familiar loss, I focused on anger. Anger I knew how to navigate. It kept me warm at night.

God, was I pathetic? Was I miserable? I knew the answer to that.

I headed downstairs. It was a madhouse. Jessica was calling orders and orchestrating the show. They stuck sticky notes on everything—bright, garish, yellow stickies.

"Mark with a Q what you'd like to keep," Jessica said, handing me a black ink pen.

I wanted everything in my childhood bedroom, the antique crystal decanter set, my mother's silver candlesticks, and my father's cherry wood desk. The rest of it didn't hold any sentimental value for me. I quickly tacked stickies to the items, and then I grabbed my coat and purse and escaped. The cold Boston air felt damp, like it was seeping into my bones. In my haste to escape, I'd forgotten my hat. The gloves were in my pockets, and I quickly whipped them out. My fingers were already cold and soon my nose was numb.

The tears came, unbidden, unwelcome. But something about the frigid outdoors felt like a safe enough place to let all the emotions I'd been holding in come oozing out. So, I cried as I walked away from my childhood home and the memories that were more a hindrance than help.

Chapter Twenty-Six

THROUGH THE ONSLAUGHT OF TEARS, I finally decided to get it together enough to call a cab. I could've called Donovan, but for some reason I didn't want him to see me like this. A mess. I didn't let anyone see the mess always lurking beneath the styled hair, the put together outfits, the makeup. This morning, I had none of my shields in place, and I knew if I looked in the mirror, I'd see red-rimmed, mascara-less eyes, rough lips that didn't even have a coating of chapstick, and I was wearing a pair of boots that were the equivalent of house slippers. Normally, I wouldn't be caught dead leaving the house less than made up, but the need to escape had been all consuming.

I couldn't feel my ears or toes by the time the cab showed up, and when I climbed into the heated interior, I shivered as I began to thaw.

"Where to?" the cabbie asked, his Boston accent thick.

"I—Can you just drive for a bit?"

He pushed a button, and the meter started to run. I burrowed into the collar of my coat as the cab pulled forward. Maybe coming back to Boston had been a terrible idea. I'd once felt like I owned the city. There wasn't a club or bar I couldn't get into, no man whose head I couldn't turn. But I came back broken and defeated—and now I was stuck here. Stuck here running my father's legacy.

I gave the cabbie the address to O'Malley Properties. The office was quiet, just what I needed. The only sound was the occasional blast of the heater. I went into my father's office—now my office—and took a seat on the leather couch. I never understood why he'd needed a couch in his office. Then again, there were many late nights and early mornings. Days when I wouldn't see my father for more than snatches of time when he'd come home to shower and change. Whenever he'd been closing a deal, he slept at the office.

My stomach rumbled, reminding me I hadn't eaten nor had any coffee or tea. But the couch looked so comfortable, and my eyes were already drooping closed. So, I curled up on the leather couch, pulled the gray Irish wool blanket over me and promptly fell asleep.

I awoke to my ringing cellphone. It was somewhere in my purse which I'd dropped next to the couch. Leaning over, I reached into the bag and pulled it out. Ori's name flashed across the screen.

Sitting up, I answered it. "Hello?"

"Hey."

"Hey." There was a dull throb hitting the temples of my skull like tiny hammers.

"Sorry if this borders on stalker behavior," he teased. "I know we had dinner last night and then I sent you a text this morning—which you never answered."

"Yeah," I sighed, leaning back against the leather cushion so my neck wouldn't have to hold my head up. "Sorry. I was dealing with some stuff this morning."

"Not regret kind of stuff, I hope."

"No. Nothing like that. My"—I swallowed, noting the difficulty of it—"stepmother came back and decided it was time to redecorate my father's home." I didn't know why I was telling him, only that I had no one else to tell. I could've called Shannon, but there was only so much misery I wanted to inflict on my best friend.

"Ah, Quinn."

That was all he said, but I understood everything he conveyed in those two words. And a part of me really liked the way he said my name. Like he owned it.

"Yeah. It wasn't a good morning."

"Where are you? Are you still at home?"

I shook my head, only realizing he couldn't see me and that it hurt. "I'm at O'Malley Properties."

"I'll be there in twenty minutes."

"You don't have to—" I said, but I was speaking to silence.

I set my phone down and then closed my eyes. I must've dozed because my phone ringing jarred me awake again. Ori calling to tell me he was downstairs.

As I gathered my coat and purse, I looked at the orchids that sat in a vase on my desk. I hadn't taken them home because I hadn't been sure I wanted them there. Wasn't sure they belonged. But now I didn't even belong in my own home.

I stumbled on my way to the elevator, my breaths shallow. As the car descended, I leaned against the panel wall and tried not to fall over. The doors opened, and I gingerly made my way through the lobby.

Ori was standing outside the glass doors, hands in his pockets, shoulders hunched against the elements.

I made sure the security system was set, and then I proceeded out into the cold.

Ori turned, his mouth agape. "Zip your coat!" His

hands immediately went to help me, but I brushed them away.

"Stop, I'm okay. I'm hot actually."

He peered at me, and then he wrapped an arm around my shoulder to guide me toward a waiting town car. Holding the door open, he gestured for me to get inside.

I slid in and immediately removed my coat and pressed a button to crack a window. Ori climbed in next to me, shut the door, and the driver peeled away from the curb. The sky was white and ominous and more snow would soon dump on the city. Boston was miserable in winter, and if you didn't have to go out in it, you wouldn't. It made me think of cold, bleak Russian winters—the ones Sasha must've endured.

How had he ever endured?

"You're flushed." Ori reached over with his palm and touched my forehead. His over familiarity didn't bother me. "Yeah, I think you have a fever, Quinn."

"Fever?" I murmured.

"How do you feel?"

"Tired—but I think that's the depression talking. My head does hurt, though. And my throat is sore." I pressed my hot face to the cool glass and breathed out a blissful sigh. "That feels nice. Where are we going?"

"My place," Ori said. "You need a bed."

"Okay."

"And soup."

I smiled even though he couldn't see me.

"No objections?" His hand reached out to gently touch my forehead again. "I don't like how hot you feel."

Closing my eyes, I continued to lean against the cool glass. "I don't have enough energy for objections."

Chapter Twenty-Seven

"QUINN," Ori said, his tone soft, as was his touch to my shoulder. "We're here."

I peeled my eyes open. Everything hurt and my tongue felt swollen in my mouth. I made a move to open the door —or tried to—but it seemed my body didn't want to listen to my brain.

"I got ya. Give me a second." He unstrapped his seatbelt, and then there was a blast of cold air as he got out of the car. I shivered and tried to hunch lower. Externally, I was freezing, but internally, I was blazing.

Ori opened the passenger side door and helped me with my seatbelt. I nearly fell out into his arms.

"Should I carry you?" he asked, not at all teasing. His dark eyes were serious with intent.

I didn't want to be touched because everything hurt all over. "No, don't carry me. I can make it."

He held out his hand and I took it, pulling myself out of the car. It was one of the hardest things I'd ever done— getting my body to work how I wanted. We took it slow up the slick sidewalk, and when we got to the front door, Ori wrapped his arm around my shoulder while he sank the key into the lock.

I stumbled into the house. Without taking his arm from around me, he guided me to a staircase. I moaned. Ori swept me into his arms and carried me up the stairs. I pressed my cheek against his chest and breathed in the smell of his wool sweater. My eyes were heavy, and incoherent thoughts tumbled through my head.

He set me down on a bed, and I instantly breathed a sigh of relief. I rolled over and tried to bring the comforter up over me, but I didn't have the strength.

"Easy," Ori said. He quickly divested me of my boots. "Christ your feet are like ice."

"Thin socks," I muttered, sinking deeper into the mattress. Either it was the most comfortable bed I'd ever been in or I was really sick.

"You need pajamas."

"I'm fine, Ori. Just let me sleep."

He didn't reply, but I did hear him moving around the room, drawers opening and closing. And then I felt him tugging at my jeans.

"Stop trying to get me naked."

Ori chuckled. "Believe me, Quinn, if I was trying to get you naked, you'd know it. Now, come on and help me out here. You'll sleep better."

I somehow managed to lift my lower half so I could slither out of my pants and into comfortable flannel pajama bottoms. Then I was able to crawl beneath the covers. The world could end, and I wouldn't have cared.

"Thanks," I whispered, not even sure if he heard me.

When I awoke again, my feet were warm, and I was sweating. I flung off the covers and then groaned when I shivered from a blast of cold air. My throat was dry and my teeth chattered.

"Hey."

I turned my head and found Ori rising from a chair next to the bed. "What are you—"

"You really should stay covered." He pulled the comforter up to my chin. "Your fever was one hundred and two the last time I checked."

"When did you check?" My voice came out in a croak.

"Right after you fell asleep. About two hours ago."

"You stuck a thermometer in my ear, and I don't remember?"

Ori shrugged, looming over me. "You were pretty out of it. How are you feeling?"

"Awful. Like the worst I've ever felt." My eyes were sore, and it hurt to keep them open. As they drifted shut, I felt a draft at my feet. "What are you doing?" I cracked one lid.

His hands were underneath the covers, and then he pulled out a hot water bottle. With a grin, he said, "I'm going to reheat this for you. It will help with breaking your fever. And then I'm bringing you some broth."

"Thank you."

"Do you want to watch some TV?"

I shook my head and then winced. A shot of pain thundered across my skull. "Is there—Can I have some water?"

Ori walked to the bedside table and picked up the bottle of water. He unscrewed the cap and then sat down on the bed next to me. I struggled to sit up, the effort exhausting.

When I was propped up against the bed frame, I reached for the bottle of water. Ori shook his head. "I got it." He helped me take a few sips and then I leaned back, breathing hard.

"Let me take your temperature again," Ori said, putting the water aside and picking up the ear thermometer. He gently placed it in my ear and pushed a button. A moment later, it beeped. He pulled it out and frowned.

"It's up a degree. Not down." He looked at me and then gently put a hand to my forehead. "Yeah, you're warmer." His hand dropped. "Let me get you that broth, okay?"

"Okay."

He set the thermometer down and then grabbed the hot water bottle. On his way to the door, he turned and stopped. "I hope you don't mind."

"Mind?"

"That I brought you here?"

"No. No I don't mind. I don't mind at all."

With a quick smile, he left the room. I closed my eyes. The throbbing in my head intensified. It hurt to move. It hurt to inhale. I rarely got sick, and when I did, I went down for the count. Sasha had never had to take care of me since I'd never been sick in the entire time we'd been together.

The door quietly opened, and Ori came back with a bowl of broth and the hot water bottle. He set the bowl of soup down on the nightstand and then lifted the covers to situate the newly heated water bottle.

"That feels wonderful." I sighed.

Ori sat down on the bed next to me and stuck the spoon in the bowl to give it a quick stir.

"I called the doctor," he said, holding out the spoon to my mouth.

The smell of chicken teased my nose, and I opened my lips for a taste, even though I had no appetite, but at the last moment I turned my head away.

"I can't," I said, trying to keep my mouth clamped shut and the sudden nausea under control.

"You need to get some fluids in you," Ori said.

"I'll drink water. Or tea. But that chicken broth…no. Please don't make me."

Ori sighed and set the bowl of soup aside. "Fine. I won't force it on you."

"Why did you call the doctor?" I asked, sliding down and tucking myself underneath the covers.

"Because your temperature is really high and I'm worried."

"It's probably just the flu. I've been stressed and—well, it's cold out. The flu is bound to happen. It's nothing to worry about."

"Well, forgive me for being a tad over protective," he said with a grim smile.

It had been a long time since I'd had someone worry about me. It made me feel warm all over, or maybe that was the fever.

Chapter Twenty-Eight

I FELT like I was burning from the inside out. Like I'd swallowed hot coals, and my organs were roasting. A cold compress touched my forehead, but I thrashed and flung it off me—along with the covers. My temperature continued to climb, and my grasp on reality slipped. Bright red lights sparkled behind my closed eyelids. Dreams I didn't remember, but when I resurfaced, lingered. Arms around me, holding me close while I whimpered and cried.

"Quinn," someone said.

It sounded like I was hearing things from underwater.

"Quinn." The voice was closer, more intense. Demanding.

I felt fingertips along my face, tracing my cheek bones.

"*Cerbiatto.*"

My eyes slowly opened—and met the dark brown, intense stare of Ori Abruzzo. He let out a slow breath, and I felt the brush of it against my skin.

Ori's fingers skated up my arms to hold my face and push away the sweat-soaked hair from my temples. My gaze darted away from him to look around the room. I couldn't tell the time, because the shades were drawn and the lamp on the bedside table was on. There was no alarm clock in the room.

"What—time? Day?" I looked at him. Ori still hadn't let go of me, but I suddenly felt back in my body and that I was completely disgusting.

"You've been in and out of it for two days." Ori's hands finally dropped from me, but he didn't get up off the bed. "The doctor came."

"Really? I don't even remember," I murmured. "Two days?"

"Two days. Your fever stayed at one hundred and four for almost that long. The doctor said you have an upper respiratory infection."

"Oh." I tried to process what he was saying. "And you… Did you stay—"

He smiled softly. "Haven't left your side."

I blinked. "Are you really the same man who called me a rich bitch cock tease?"

"You're never going to let me live that down, are you?"

"You have to admit," I said, swiping my dry lips with my tongue, "you were a major ass."

"You found me attractive. Admit it."

"Absolutely," I said, not even denying it.

"Wow, you just surprised the hell out of me."

"Lying to you after you've been taking care of me would make me a bitch. Wouldn't you agree?"

He chuckled. "Your words, not mine."

"I need some water," I said. "And I definitely could use a bath."

"I'll say."

I cringed. "That bad, right?"

"Honestly? Yeah. You don't look like your normal self."

His thumb traced my cheekbone. "You've lost weight. I can tell. I don't like it."

"Ori," I whispered.

"Don't say anything, Quinn. Not now. Okay? Let's just get you into a bath, and I'll make you some broth. You need broth."

I closed one eye and stared at him. "Didn't you already try to feed me chicken broth?"

"I did. You refused. Don't worry, I won't try that again. I've got something else for you."

"Water. Then bathing. Then food."

Ori handed me a glass and I chugged the cool water. When I finished, I was panting. I set it aside.

"I must be feeling better," I told him as he helped me up from the putrid sheets. "I can't think of anything besides a bath."

Ori led me into the guest bathroom, a large room with a separate shower and tub. He helped me over to the toilet and urged me to sit down. Then he crouched down by the tub and turned on the faucet.

"How hot do you want it?" he asked, hand underneath the flowing water.

"Luke warm, please." I was feeling light-headed. I wondered how I was supposed to bathe myself. I was as weak as a newborn kitten.

As the water was running, Ori stood and then raked a hand through his disheveled hair. I noticed his blue dress shirt was wrinkled and untucked, his slacks in need of a dry cleaner. And his jaw was covered in dark stubble.

"You didn't leave my bedside," I stated.

He put his hand to the sink. "No, I didn't."

The bags under his eyes were suddenly pronounced. I licked my dry lips. "Why?"

"Why? What do you mean, why?"

"I mean, you had a doctor come to examine me. I'm sure you could've hired a nurse. But you stayed. Why?"

"Because I care about you."

"But why?" I asked again. "You hardly know me."

"Despite your tough exterior and your adamant refusal to let me in, I'm convinced you need me."

"Need you? I don't need anyone," I scoffed.

"Do you really believe that?"

"People have let me down. Including my own family."

His dark eyes remained on me. "I'm not most people, Quinn. So stop expecting that I'm going to disappoint you."

I swallowed. Ori turned away from me and turned off the water. "Time for a bath."

"You are not going to watch me undress."

"If I didn't think you'd fall over, I'd have no problem leaving you. But I'm afraid if I leave you to your own devices, you'd drown."

I wasn't a modest individual. Hell, I'd gone topless in Saint-Tropez, and I'd sat naked in a vat of vodka for a magazine ad. Modest, I wasn't. But vulnerable was something I just didn't do. Not anymore.

"I'll call if I need your help."

He stared at me for a long moment and then he nodded. "I'll be right outside that door."

"I won't call for you," I warned. "Even if I'm drowning."

Ori stalked over to me and leaned over so he was eye level with me. "You make life very interesting." He chucked me under the chin and then walked out of the bathroom.

The man was a puzzle I couldn't figure out. I had more walls than the city of Troy, and like the Greeks, Ori was determined to scale them. Yet he was Italian. Okay, maybe that metaphor didn't work. I needed food.

"Men love a challenge!" I yelled.

"You're not a challenge, Quinn. You're special, and I'm not an idiot so I recognize it. Only an idiot would let a treasure slip through his fingers. Now get in the bath and let me imagine you naked."

A startled laugh escaped my mouth. Despite my lack of energy and that I was winded walking from the toilet to the tub, I was in good spirits.

Somehow I managed to get my clothes off and step into the bath without falling over. I moaned and slid under the water. Knowing I only had a finite amount of time before my energy disappeared completely, I quickly washed my hair and body. When the water was cool, I did one final rinse and then stood. I reached for the towel hanging on the rack next to the tub, but lightheadedness took over, and I leaned against the wall.

Breathing deeply, I concentrated on not falling. I barely registered the knock on the door. If I didn't say something, Ori wouldn't go away—he'd burst into the room.

"I'll be right out," I called. I tried to move my arms, but found I couldn't make them work. With all my effort, I grabbed the towel with one hand, but it slipped through my fingers and fell to the floor.

"Quinn? Are you okay?"

Sighing, I closed my eyes. "I need help."

No one could ever say that my pride felled me.

I kept my eyes closed as I heard the door open. "Christ," Ori muttered. A moment later, I felt the bath towel around me, and then I was being lifted out of the tub.

"I'm not a God damn saint, ya know?" he muttered as he carried me into the bedroom. He set me down in the chair and then stepped away. "Will you be okay if I change the sheets?"

I nodded.

Ori began to strip the bed, and then he disappeared out of the room. When he came back, he was carrying a spare set of clean gray sheets.

"You don't have people who do this for you?" I asked as he tucked the sheet under one corner of the mattress.

"You assume all criminals have paid help?"

"Kinda yeah," I teased. "How else would they have time to game the system?"

He shoved a pillow into its case. "It really doesn't bother you that I—have alternate business practices?"

I shivered as the water droplets on my skin began to dry. "It would be hypocritical, don't you think? To reap the rewards of my father's enterprises and then pass judgment?"

"I normally have help," Ori admitted. He finished making the bed and then went to the dresser to pull out another set of spare pajamas. "But you were sick and I didn't want you to be disturbed." He looked at me and held up the pajamas.

"Ah, I don't have a spare set of clean underwear." For some reason, that idea made me blush.

"Oh." He chuckled, looking oddly nervous, too. "If you don't mind a set of boxers, I have a pair I could give you. They're silk."

"Of course they are. And yes, that would be nice."

Any other time, I would've gone commando and not worried about it. But I was sick and when you're sick, you wanted different levels of comfort. While Ori was gone, I managed to get into the button up pajama tops. I was just wrapping the towel around my waist when he returned. He handed me a pair of navy blue, silk boxer briefs and then like a gentleman, turned around.

"Okay," I said, pulling up the pajama bottoms. "I'm decent."

He turned and grinned. "I—never mind."

"No, come on, say it."

Ori pulled back the covers of the bed and gestured for me to climb in. "I was just thinking how much I liked the idea of you wearing my underwear, but then I thought that would sound kinky and weird."

I laughed, oddly content and sleepy. "They're comfortable. Thank you."

He went to the bedside table and picked up a remote. When he pressed a button, the walls over the dresser opened to reveal a television screen. Ori pressed another button, and the TV flared to life.

"What would you like to watch? The news?"

"Oh, God no."

He chuckled. "I was kidding. I've got HBO. Stars?"

"*Outlander* reruns? Sign me up."

"Ah, you have a thing for the Scots?"

I snorted. "Hardly."

Maybe I should've asked him to find *Dr. Zhivago*. Lack of food was definitely getting to me.

"What is your thing, Quinn, because I'm trying to figure it out, and I just can't read you?"

"Are you asking if I like you, Ori?" I teased, leaning my wet head against the pillow. I should've taken the time to comb out my hair, but it was going to dry weird anyway so what was the point?

Ori wormed his hand underneath the covers, seeking mine out. When he found my hand, he laced his fingers through mine.

"Do you like me, Quinn?" His brown eyes delved into mine.

I'd seen him as an arrogant, know it all, brash man.

Now all I saw was a rumpled one. He hadn't shaved in days. He hadn't left my side. And he hadn't cracked any jokes about having to come into the bathroom to help me out of the tub.

"You're not all you seem to be. You know that, don't you?" I asked quietly.

He stared at me for a long moment and then pulled our joined hands out from underneath the comforter. He brought them to his lips and kissed the back of my hand. It was the only time he'd ever kissed me—and if I hadn't been feeling so rotten, or worried about my breath, I would've asked him to kiss me.

I wasn't bold enough to kiss him myself.

Ori made me feel like an unsure teenager. It was both a blessing and curse.

Chapter Twenty-Nine

I FOUND a *Seinfeld* rerun and settled in to watch while Ori was downstairs heating me some soup. I wondered what he was going to bring me since chicken was definitely out.

Jerry was in the middle of cracking a good one-liner when Ori walked back into the room, carrying a tray.

"Beef?" I asked in surprise, sniffing the air.

"Bone broth," he said. "Mama's recipe. Her bread recipe too." He gestured to the thick slices of bread on the plate.

"Did you make all this?" I wondered. "How could you have made it if you haven't left my side."

A slight blush stained his cheeks. "Ah no. I didn't make it. Mama did."

I blinked. "Mama? Your mother is here?"

"She might be here," he admitted.

"When did she arrive?"

Ori looked at the bowl of bone broth. "The day after I brought you here."

"Ori," I warned. "What the hell is going on?"

"Eat," he commanded. "You eat and I'll talk."

I gave him the stink eye but reached for a slice of the bread. I tore a piece and then dunked it into the bone marrow broth. I let it soak for a moment and then popped it into my mouth.

"Jesus, Mary and Joseph," I whispered. "That's the best thing I've ever had."

He grinned. "Normally, I would chalk it up to the fact that you haven't eaten in two days, but I know how good these recipes are."

"Your mother," I prompted as I dunked another piece.

"I called her after you wouldn't eat the chicken soup. Before I knew what was happening, she was on a train bound for Boston."

"Your mother came all the way from—wait, where is she from?"

"New York—Brooklyn. It's where I grew up."

"Oh. Oh, I see." Ori's mother was here. In this house. Where I was sick. That seemed…wow.

He nodded. "And she didn't barge in here to take care of you. Which actually shows restraint on her part."

"Why would she want to take care of me?" I asked in confusion.

"It's what she does. She's everyone's mother. I…had a friend. Growing up. Motherless. She sort of adopted him." His eyes darkened with a memory I wasn't privy to. He glanced back at me and smiled, the memory fading. "Anyway, you get a mother whether you want one or not. And the moment I tell her you're well enough, she's gonna barge in here and feed you until you explode.

I smiled. "That sounds nice, actually. It's been a while since…well, since I had…"

I devoured the broth and bread. When I was full, I leaned back, feeling my eyes drifting shut.

Ori lifted the tray and stood up. He moved toward the door. "Get some rest," he said.

"Will you come back?" I blurted out.

He looked at me over his shoulder. "You want me to come back?"

"I mean, you don't have to. You probably want a shower and your own bed, some time to yourself. But, if for some reason, you don't want that—the time to yourself, I mean. Well, it would be okay if you came back."

"But you'll be asleep," he pointed out.

"Yeah."

"And you're sick."

"You think I'm disgusting."

He raised his eyebrows. "Disgusting? Hardly."

"Then why are you making this so hard for me?"

Ori set the tray on the dresser and then came over to sit on the bed. "I don't trust you."

"Me? You don't *trust* me?" It was hard to be indignant from a bed, but somehow I made it work.

"When you're healthy, you're ready for battle. All the time. Your defenses are up and you don't let anyone in."

"I let people in," I interrupted.

He gave me a look that said he knew better. "Maybe. I called your best friend, and she wanted to come to your side, but I told her not to worry about it because I was going to take care of you."

"Shannon's pregnant. She shouldn't have offered—"

Ori placed a hand over my lips. "Would you please let me talk?" I nodded and he dropped his hand. "You don't like being vulnerable, and right now, I seem to be all you have. And I admit that I like it. I like taking care of you. I like pretending that you need me. But what happens when your fever breaks for good and you fight off the infection. You're going to get up and leave and go back to being

Quinn O'Malley, the woman who doesn't need anyone. I just don't— I can't—I don't want that. But I know you'll do that. So, no Quinn, I don't trust you to stay vulnerable and to let me in."

He stared at me for a long moment, and then he got up, took the tray, and left. The bed was comfortable, the room was quiet, and I suddenly didn't like that he was gone.

I'd built walls around myself, hoping that kept others out. All it did was close me in. I was suffocating, slowly. So slowly I hadn't noticed I wasn't really living, just existing from one moment to the next.

I wanted to talk to someone. But not Shannon or Adam. Not even Barrett. Maybe I'd been doing the wrong type of talking. I sent a text to someone who could be objective, someone who could be blunt, someone whom I should've continued talking to after my father had died. But like everything else in my life, I'd let it fall through the cracks.

There was a knock on the door and then a moment later, a gray-haired head popped in. The woman smiled, her face creased.

"You're awake. Good." She came in, carrying a plate of cannoli.

"You must be Ori's mother," I said with a winsome smile.

"I am." She set the plate down in front of me and then moved her plump form to the same chair her son had sat in. She gestured to the dessert. "Eat."

I picked up the Italian custard pastry and took a bite. It was delicious, but it wasn't like I expected it to be anything else.

"You are feeling better?" she asked as she rested her hands in her lap.

I nodded and continued to eat.

"My son. He likes you. A lot."

I choked on the custard and then managed to swallow it down.

"Do you like him?"

Abruzzos had honesty in spades, apparently.

"I—yes. I like him."

She peered at me with shrewd eyes. "There are many types of like. Which kind is it?"

Heat climbed up my cheeks. Was my fever back? I pressed a hand to my forehead, not that I could tell, but it felt cool. "I don't know."

The door to the bedroom opened and Ori strode in and stopped. "Mama, what are you—"

"Hush, Ori. I'm having a talk with your friend."

Ori groaned and then said something in Italian. She fired something back. He used hand gestures and a pleading tone. Mama Abruzzo sighed and then stood. "All right, all right. I'll let you handle it." She patted his cheek and then looked at me. She smiled and then she left.

"Sorry," Ori muttered.

"About what?" I asked in amusement, enjoying his discomfort.

"About whatever Mama said. She has no boundaries."

"Yes, I realize that." I gestured to the other cannoli on the plate. "Do you want it? I'm full."

He glanced at the door. "Don't let my mother hear you say that. She won't let people leave her table with anything left on their plates." Ori quickly scooped up the cannoli and closed his eyes in delight.

"You came back," I said, noting the change of clothes and his damp hair. He hadn't shaved though, and the stubble was thicker on his chin.

He swallowed before answering. "I don't think I was fair."

"You were completely fair," I insisted. "And not at all out of line. I don't like—I wish—" I sighed. "I loved someone once. Very deeply. And when he left, it shattered me so completely I wasn't sure I was ever going to be myself again."

Ori's dark brown eyes were intense, unwavering. "Why did he leave?"

My gaze slipped from him. I stared at the gray coverlet as I thought about the letter Sasha had written for me. "He was in an accident—a fire. Badly burned. Near death. He wanted to die. Much to his surprise, he lived. He was bedridden for the better part of a year. Angry. Bitter. Mean. But I didn't care, because I loved him. None of it mattered to me, Ori. Not his charred flesh, not the hair that refused to grow back on the right side of his head. I didn't care about any of that. I looked at him and still saw *him*. But he couldn't. He just…couldn't." I swallowed. I hadn't said this much about Sasha to a stranger ever. And now I was spewing our story, laying it at Ori's feet, wondering if he would pick it up and examine it. Or realize he was better off without me.

"He eventually healed enough to get out of bed, to laugh with me, to—to make love to me—and I thought, *finally* he's back. My love came back. But one morning, I woke up to a note and he was gone."

"Gone," he repeated quietly.

"Gone. I woke up in our Manhattan apartment we shared, surrounded by all his things that he didn't take with him." I looked at him and smiled sadly. "Broke every dish and glass in the place. And then I came back to Boston."

I left out a lot, of course. Who Sasha was. Why he'd been in the fire. I couldn't bring myself to tell Ori about the baby. Not yet. Maybe one day. But that was a raw wound that wasn't healing, not even with time. The scab of Sasha's abandonment, the scab of my father's death— those were diminishing each day, little by little. But not the baby. Not my son.

"Quinn?"

"Yeah, Ori?"

"Can I climb into bed with you and hold you?"

I snuggled back under the blanket, but moved it aside, just enough to give Ori space to crawl into bed next to me. He pulled me into his arms. I pressed my cheek to his body and fell asleep to the rise and fall of his chest.

Chapter Thirty

"I HAVE TO GO HOME," I said three days later.

"Why?" Ori asked. He was currently pressing his body on top of mine, his fingers were in my hair, and his mouth was dangerously close to mine. We'd been dancing around our first kiss, both knowing it was coming closer to the moment when he'd place his lips on mine.

I put my hands to his stomach and tried to push him off me. He lifted himself ever so slightly so I could breathe, but he refused to move.

"I like having you here," he said.

I liked being there. But I didn't say that to him. Ori had given me a tour of the place. The street was quiet, and I didn't hear any traffic. The house was two-stories but modest. Nothing like the house I'd grown up in. Nothing like the warehouse loft I'd shared with Sasha. Rich browns and earth tones, modern, without being cold. Like you expected an Italian grandmother to come out of the kitchen wearing an apron and brandishing a wooden spoon.

"I need my own clothes," I told him. For the last three

days I'd been wearing his silk boxer briefs. Couldn't say I was at all disappointed, but still, I missed the expensive lace I normally wore.

"We can get you your clothes."

"If I eat another meal of your mother's, I won't be able to fit into my normal clothes."

His hand trailed down my body and then grasped my hip, and he shifted so I felt him in the cleft between my legs. "You're beautiful. And you were too thin even before you got sick."

The feeling of him pressed up against me had me drunk with desire. It had been so long since a man had touched me. It had been so long since I'd *wanted* a man to touch me.

"I gave you a toothbrush," he whispered, coming closer. "I've seen you sweaty and sick, I've seen you without makeup or your hair styled, and you know what?"

"What?" I panted.

"I like you naked."

His lips captured mine. Rough, lust-soaked, needy. Like both of us had been waiting for this moment since forever. I came alive from his kiss, a dying bloom suddenly stretching open, seeking the sun.

My hands sank into his hair as I tilted my head, wanting his lips on mine for as long as I could draw breath. I was consumed, starving. Starving for more. Starving for all of it. For everything I hadn't felt in two years. The walls around my heart started to crumble as I shook with desire.

Ori rolled us so that he was on his back, and I was sprawled on top of him. I pulled back to stare down at him. His dark eyes swam with intention, with passion. His thumb came up to graze my swollen bottom lip.

"I just want to bury myself in you," he rasped, his breathing escalated. "If I asked, would you let me?"

His words had me shivering, and just as I was about to answer, there was a knock on the door.

"Quinn?"

At the sound of my name, I rolled off of Ori onto the floor. "Ow," I muttered, my head clearing of lust as my bum throbbed from landing hard.

The door opened. "Mama," Ori growled. "What is it?"

"Don't take that tone with me," she said lightly. Her gaze strayed to me—I was still on the floor—and she smiled. "Did I interrupt something?"

"No," I said at the exact time Ori said, "Yes."

Mama Abruzzo laughed. "Dinner's ready." She left, closing the door on her way.

I put my hands on the bed and pushed myself up. "I can't believe you let me sit on the floor. You didn't even try and help me up."

Ori glanced at his lap. "I'm having a bit of my own problem, Quinn."

I let out a giggle—*a giggle*. I never giggled. And yet, here I was, sounding like a teenaged-girl who had just gotten caught by her boyfriend's mother. That word sobered me really fast.

"Oh, God, Quinn, don't," Ori growled and then reached out. He grasped my hand and pulled me onto the bed. "You are not allowed to freak out."

"How did—"

"I've got your number, Quinn." He smiled. "And don't even think about trying to shake me off."

I gave him a wobbly smile. "I'll have dinner, but then I need to go home."

"We're back to that? Why do you have to go home? Didn't you say that your stepmother is redecorating?"

"Yes. I did say that."

"And do you really want to be there while she deconstructs your childhood home?"

"No." The thought of not having my childhood home depressed me but not enough to fight for it. It was just a place. "I have friends I can stay with."

"Your friend Shannon?" he pressed. "Your *pregnant* friend Shannon?"

"I have other friends," I stated. "Adam and Richard. And their baby daughter, Hannah." I shook my head as Ori's smile grew.

"Just stay here. For a few more days. Use the time to find your own apartment," he suggested.

"I have an appointment tomorrow. I can't miss it. And I've been out of the office for a few days. I haven't even called to check in—"

"Go to your appointment. Go to work. I'm not stopping you from living your life, Quinn. I'm just saying that I enjoy having you here, and I'd like it if you came back. That's all."

"I'm not ready to have sex with you."

"Noted."

"You gave in rather easily," I pointed out.

"Oh, I still plan on trying to get into your pants, don't worry." Ori got up off the bed and stood to face me. "So what do you say? Will you stay?"

I pretended to think about it, but really, there was nothing to consider. I felt good around Ori. Smiling, I nodded. "I'll stay. But on one condition."

"What's that?"

"You find a tactful way to tell your mother to stop feeding me."

Ori reached out to grasp my arm and pulled me to him, until we both fell over onto the bed. "I'll do one better. I'll tell Mama she can head home."

"You can't kick out your own mother."

"I'm not kicking her out. Trust me. She'll want to go."

"Why?"

His hand touched my cheek, and he smiled. "Ask me again. Later."

I frowned in confusion. "I don't understand."

"I'd tell you, but it would just freak you out. So I'm not planning on scaring you off, okay? Let's go down to dinner."

Sighing, I nodded. "What are we having?"

"Pasta. Probably."

"Remind me to go shopping tomorrow too. For bigger pants."

"If you date an Italian, you have to be prepared," he warned. He held my hand as we left the bedroom.

"Dating? Is that what we're doing?"

"Yes, Quinn. That's what we're doing."

I held in a smile. "All right."

"You're amenable?"

"It all hinges on the size of pants I buy tomorrow."

Chapter Thirty-One

I LOOKED out the large glass window at the Boston streets below. Downtown was bustling. It wasn't one of those cities that stopped because of the weather. Some of the nicest days occurred during the winter. Bright blue skies and sunshine. Like today. Today was gorgeous. Though maybe it wasn't all due to the weather.

"I was surprised to hear from you." Dr. Waverly Anderson sat in a leather-backed chair, her dark hair elegantly coiffed. Her gaze was shrewd and observant. Not at all judgmental. I'd been her patient for a decade. On and off. I'd gone to see her for a few months after my mother had died when I just hadn't been able to connect with the world. Pills were a last resort for her, and she didn't prescribe them cavalierly.

I'd taken them after losing the baby.

"Yeah, I kind of surprised myself." I turned to look at her and smiled.

"Do you want to sit?" She gestured to the leather couch that matched her chair. Her office didn't feel like an office. If anything, it reminded me of an old English library. Her practice was in an old Boston brownstone.

"I'll sit," I said, walking over to the couch and plopping down.

"I like your hair. It's a nice change."

My hand reached up to touch the shortened locks. "I thought it was time, you know?"

She nodded, her hands folded in her lap. She never took notes when we spoke. It felt less patient/doctor and more friend to friend. A friend with a PhD in clinical psychology and an MD in Psychiatry.

"How are you?" she asked.

"I"—I inhaled a deep breath—"I'm doing well."

She smiled. "That's good."

"I'm dating."

"Glad to hear it."

I paused and looked at my lap. My gray slacks were pressed, and my black cashmere turtleneck was elegantly casual since I was prepared to spend the rest of the day in the office catching up on work.

"But?" Waverly said.

Looking up, I smiled. "How did you know there was a but coming?"

"You wouldn't have made an appointment if it was all sunshine and roses. Am I right?"

"You're right." I sighed. "He's…intense. Ori. And he… Why does it have to be all or nothing?"

"What do you mean?"

"Well, like with Sasha." I nearly tripped over his name. I wondered if there would ever be a time that I could say his name and not emotionally falter. "We met and that was it. We were together. With Ori…I don't want to jump into something like that again."

"So don't."

I blinked. "Yeah. If only it was that easy."

"Have you slept with him?"

"If you're going to ask questions like that, then I should've come at cocktail hour," I teased.

"Quinn. You're deflecting."

"Ah, just when I was beginning to think you were a different type of therapist." I shook my head. "No, we haven't slept together."

"Is he pressuring you?"

My face softened. "Not at all."

"Did you tell him about Sasha?"

"I told him a little bit about Sasha. About the accident and why he left."

"And the baby? Did you tell him about your son?"

I swallowed, feeling my eyes fill with tears. Not a lot made me cry. Talking about my son, though. That split me open. "No."

"Will you?"

"I don't know if I can."

"Why do you keep it so close to you?" she asked.

I got up from the couch and went over to the window again. White clouds that hadn't been in the sky an hour ago were now rolling in. More snow would be coming.

Why didn't I talk about the baby? Maybe because the father had never known he'd existed. Because thinking of the baby and Sasha in one place made me want to rip my heart from my chest so it never beat in pain again.

"It happened," Waverly said gently. "Not talking about that doesn't change it."

"Talking about it doesn't change that either."

I'd written Sasha a letter. Many letters. Some were stained with tears of grief. Some were stained with tears of rage. He'd left me. He'd left our son. He hadn't been there when he died. He hadn't been there when I'd almost died.

"Letting someone in doesn't make you weak, Quinn. It actually makes you strong."

Turning, I pinned her with my stare. "How do you figure?"

"Letting someone in means you're giving life—and love—a chance. So you can say all you want that you're dating. And maybe you are. Maybe this guy is someone you want to share your life with. But how will you know if you keep your deepest secret from him." She paused. "Do you trust him?"

"I trusted someone before," I pointed out. "And he left me. Left us."

"Sasha leaving had nothing to do with you. You know that. On some level."

"Every man that has ever meant anything to me has left me, Waverly. Sean, Dad, Sasha. What the hell do I do with that?"

"So you're waiting for Ori to leave you, too. Is that it? You want him to leave you now because if he does, it'll be less painful. But it would also prove you right. That you shouldn't trust, shouldn't love. People die. Hearts break. You're still standing, Quinn. But don't you want more? You could have more."

"The fear never really goes away," I said softly. "Sometimes, I manage to bury it so deep. I just don't know if I could survive another loss."

"But what if you take just one more risk? One more risk. A bet is never a sure thing. You're twenty-seven years old, and you're acting like an eighty-year-old widow. It's like you're waiting around for the end of your life. I'd hate to see you waste it, the time you've been given."

I glanced at her left hand. A simple gold wedding band encircled her ring finger. "It's easy to tell me to be happy, isn't it?"

"You're making assumptions," Waverly said. "Because you see a wedding band you think I have everything you don't, so I can tell you to be happy. To choose happiness." She took off her ring, reached behind her, and stuck it on her desk. "Will this make it easier for you? Are you now willing to listen to my advice?"

"Everyone thinks they know better than I do. They think—"

"*They* who?"

"The people closest to me. All of them are married with children. Or children on the way."

"What advice have they been offering you?"

"Unsolicited," I quipped. "They seem to all have an opinion on how to move forward, that I should move forward. Date."

"Well, you are dating, aren't you?"

"Can it be considered dating if it's just one person?" I said.

She cocked her head to one side. "Do you have any interest in meeting someone else? Dating around?"

"I really don't."

"So, again, I have to ask, why are you really here? Are you looking for approval? You don't want to jump into something with one man, yet you're reluctant to play the field."

"I've played the field," I retorted.

"Partying like a rock star and sleeping with the city's most eligible is not playing the field."

"I haven't done that since I was nineteen," I reminded her. Nineteen and trying to prove that I could do just fine without a mother and with a father who had refused to give me boundaries. Until he'd threatened to yank me out of college and throw me into rehab. It had been the wakeup call both of us had needed. My father had realized he needed to be a *father*.

"That's my point, Quinn." Waverly's forceful tone had softened. "You aren't who you used to be. You're not the wild teen. You're not even the woman who fell in love with Sasha. You're allowed to change, you're allowed to want different things, make different choices. I'm going to ask you a question."

"Joy," I muttered.

Waverly smiled. "Well, maybe you're still a little bit of the old Quinn." I laughed as she went on, "Does being with Ori make you happy?"

"Yes."

"Does he make you feel good about yourself?"

"I'm not sure."

"Okay, let me put it another way. Do you find yourself making good decisions with him around?"

I thought back to our short time together. Most of our time had been him taking care of me while I recovered from an upper respiratory infection. A lot of my choices had been in his hands. But I found that I was going to bed without that glass of vodka.

"What if he's a crutch?" I asked.

"What do you do when you're together?"

"We talk. We joke. We laugh."

"And you're not intimate yet, right?"

I shook my head. This was the slowest I'd ever taken a relationship.

"I think it's safe to say that he's not a crutch. When you think of a happy, healthy relationship, what do you envision?"

"My parents," I said. It was automatic and not even something I had to think about. "They loved each other. They were best friends. They supported each other. And even when they fought, it wasn't an all out screaming match. None of this name-calling. None of this saying things just to hurt the other person."

"What was your relationship with Sasha like?"

No longer wishing to stand, I moved back to the couch and took a seat. I leaned back against the leather and closed my eyes. "It was…everything. It was exciting, but safe. It was full of passion, but commitment. He was faithful. Physically anyway. But emotionally…in the beginning, he was in love with another woman. No. Not in love." I fell silent, trying to search for the words. "Barrett was his family. He loved her. He would've done anything for her, but he respected her husband too much to ever cross the line."

"Sounds complicated."

"Very." I nodded and then I smiled in remembrance.

"What's that smile about?"

"The night I met Barrett. She called me a bitch. To Sasha. Behind my back, but I'd heard it. Witnessed it." I shook my head. "We were in Las Vegas, celebrating the opening of Barrett's husband's hotel. I left Sasha there. Didn't tell him where I'd gone. Just flew back to Boston."

"Did he come after you?"

"Immediately." My face colored with amusement. "The next night, I went out with a friend—a male friend and gay—but Sasha didn't realize that. He stormed into the restaurant where I was having dinner. He would've slugged Adam, but I stood up, put my hand on his chest, and shoved him out of the dining room."

We'd yelled at each other in the street, not caring that others could hear our fight.

You hurt me. When you chose her, I'd said.

I want to choose you. If you let me, he'd replied.

I wasn't sure I'd understood what he meant by that.

"So what happened?" Waverly asked, jarring me out of the past.

I blinked, the smell of the Boston street in the evening disappearing. "I let him in. But it wasn't all resolved, you know? Barrett and I came to an understanding one night and eventually we became friends."

But everything changed once again when Sasha was in the accident. Badly burned, in pain. He'd asked Barrett to kill him. To put him out of his misery. The strange part? I wasn't upset that he'd wanted to die—I was upset that he hadn't asked me to do it for him. That in his hour of need he'd turned to her.

When the plan had gone awry, and Sasha had no choice but to recover, he told me why he'd asked her. He didn't want his death on my conscience. He didn't want me to have to carry that with me the rest of my life. He'd wanted to keep me innocent—well, as innocent as the daughter of a criminal could be.

What he hadn't realized was that if he'd died in that hospital bed, I would've blamed myself anyway. It had been my fault he'd gotten hurt. My fault for the burning of his flesh. If I hadn't been so stupid. If I'd paid more attention, I never would've been used as bait. Because Sasha's enemies knew he'd come for me.

"Quinn?" came Waverly's voice.

"Yeah?" My eyes cleared of the past, my past that was always so close to my present.

"I think that's enough for today."

Chapter Thirty-Two

I THOUGHT therapy was supposed to make a person feel better. Waverly wasn't a coddler, which was why I chose to see her in the first place. But I hadn't expected the trip down memory lane. The long windy road down memory lane, plagued with thorns. My session with her hadn't given me any true clarity.

She'd been right; I had been looking for validation that the choices I was making were, indeed, healthy ones. I wasn't good at letting go of the past. I held on to memories, clung to them. Probably longer than I should. Using them as an excuse not to move forward. Being aware of your behavior was the first step, but it wasn't like I was going to change who I was overnight. I wasn't suddenly healed and happy, ready to let Ori in because I'd talked to my shrink that had known me for a decade.

With a shake of my head, I walked into O'Malley Properties and greeted the security guard on duty.

"Are you feeling better, Ms. O'Malley?" Bernie asked.

"You knew I was sick?" I cocked my head to the side, holding in a frown.

He nodded. "Beverly told me."

"Did she," I murmured. It wasn't Beverly's business to spread the news of my illness around the office. If I was out of the office, I was out of the office. End of discussion.

"Have a nice day, Ms. O'Malley. Glad you're feeling better."

I smiled at him, grateful for his concern. "Thank you, Bernie." I strolled through the lobby to the elevators and pushed the button. A moment later, the doors dinged and then opened. I rode up the many floors, deep in thought about how I was going to handle the situation with Beverly. I'd been tip-toeing around the issue, not wanting to throw my weight around, not wanting to seem like the spoiled daughter of Michael O'Malley who wanted to come in and change everything.

But maybe it was time.

My father was never coming back. He'd left me his business, and it was time to use my knowledge of the city —along with my youth—to my advantage.

As the elevator doors opened, I squared my shoulders and strode across the top floor of the building. The view through the large glass windows never ceased to amaze me. I understood why powerful people paid for views. It made them feel like they sat in the clouds and owned the world. I took that feeling and harnessed it.

The office was quiet since most people were out to lunch, but Beverly sat at her desk. She ate her sandwich as she flipped through a glossy magazine. She looked up, mouth forming an O of surprise. She jumped to her feet. "Ms. O'Malley! You're here."

I arched an eyebrow. "I told you I would be."

Color suffused her cheeks. Bobbing her head, she resembled a terrified chicken. "Right."

"Will you come into my office, please?" I didn't wait for

her reply. I opened the closed door to my father's—my—office. After shrugging out of my coat and hanging it on the coat rack in the corner, I went behind the massive desk and took a seat.

Beverly came through the door and stopped.

I looked up at her. "Close the door, please, and have a seat."

With a resigned look, she sat her plump form into the chair across from me. I picked up my father's fountain pen, taking comfort in the weight of it. It made me feel close to him. I knew the letter he'd left me—the letter with no instructions—had been written with that pen.

"You don't like me, do you?" I asked.

Beverly flinched as if I'd yelled the question. "I like you," she lied.

I swirled in the chair, just enough so that I could cross my leg over the other. "How long have you worked here?"

"Ten years."

"Ten years," I repeated. "Did you like working for my father?"

"I did." Her chin lifted as if daring me to contradict her.

"Why?"

"Why?" She blinked brown owlish eyes.

"Yes. Tell me why you liked working for my father."

"He was a good boss. He always remembered my birthday."

When she paused, I frowned. "That's all? That's all it took for him to be a good boss to you?"

"He asked my opinions," she threw out. "He asked my opinions on projects and designs. He made me feel…" She shrugged. "Useful. Now," she said, pinning me with a stare, "I sit at my desk and eat sandwiches while I direct incoming calls."

"Beverly," I began. "Your hostility toward me has been prevalent since the moment I walked into this office. You didn't offer to help me—with anything. Instead, you glared at me like it was my fault my father had died. I was hoping you'd come around. But as I can see now, working together isn't a good idea."

"Excuse me?"

"I'm prepared to offer you a very generous severance package." I leaned back in my father's office chair and watched the woman's face slacken in shock.

"You're *firing* me?" she spat.

"You've made it clear you don't like me," I pointed out, without any heat in my tone. "And furthermore, you told Bernie I was out because I was sick."

"You *were* sick!"

"Discretion, Beverly. You have no discretion. You may not like me, but I don't trust you."

Trust. That word again kept popping up in my life. I wasn't great at trusting people, but I trusted my gut. At least when it came to Beverly.

The woman rose from the chair, her skin blotchy with indignation. "You're a spoiled bitch, and you're going to ruin this company!" She stalked to the door, flung it open, and marched out.

I didn't move until I was sure she was gone, and then I called down to Bernie to get the key from Beverly. I knew vindictive women. I'd grown up around them. I recognized the signs. Beverly might've claimed to be loyal to my father, which was why she'd treated me with such vitriol, but it was only a thinly veiled excuse.

There was a knock on my open door, and a man in his forties stood in the doorway. He was dressed casually with rolled up sleeves and horn-rimmed glasses on his nose.

Setting the phone down, I waved him in. "Hey, Jimmy."

He smiled. "Hey ya, Ms. O'Malley."

I rolled my eyes. "You used to call me Quinn."

"You didn't used to be my boss," he teased. "What happened to Beverly? I saw her stomp out of here in a rage."

"I fired her."

Jimmy raised his dark eyebrows. "Did you now? That's interesting."

"You don't look surprised."

He set a folder down in front of me. "We were all taking bets actually—about how long she'd last."

I leaned back in my chair and didn't reach for the folder. "You're kidding. There was an office pool going on?"

Jimmy scratched his jaw and had the grace to look sheepish. "Ah, yeah. Beverly didn't really keep her feelings to herself. So we all wondered when you'd give her the ax."

Shaking my head, I tried to cover my smile and failed. "What other bets are going on?"

He straightened his spine. "No other bets."

"Jimmy."

"I'm an architect, Ms. O'Malley. I stay in my office, I design, and I ignore any and all gossip."

"Uh huh."

"You want me to be labeled the office snitch?" he demanded.

"You want to win the pools or what? You have to give me a heads up."

"You'd *fix* the pools?" He leaned forward.

"For a piece of the pie. Sure."

Jimmy laughed. "Hustler!"

I chuckled. "Come on, tell me. I won't be mad."

"Well," he said, sobering, "there's only one other pool going. And it's not a funny one."

"What is it?"

He had the grace to look uncomfortable. "People are taking bets on when you'll sell the company."

I picked up my father's pen, held it in my hand. "They'll be waiting a long time for that."

"Good."

"Do you mean that, Jimmy, or are you just bullshitting me?"

"No bullshit, Ms. O'Malley."

"For the love of God, call me Quinn. And spread the word around the office for people to call me Quinn."

"I'll do my best. But…"

"But?" I demanded. "But what?"

"They're all a little afraid of you."

"Why?"

"You're kidding right?" he asked in surprise. "You didn't know?"

"How would I know that?"

He shook his head. "Wow. Okay."

"Continue, please."

"We just—we're still trying to come to grips with Michael's passing. And you came in, took over, which we all didn't expect. So even though we knew you, recognized you, hell, some of us watched you grow up—I think a lot of us were expecting the girl we knew."

"The wild teen, you mean. The party girl."

He shrugged and then nodded. "Yeah, I guess. And when you weren't that, like you actually walked in here with a brain and a purpose, it just kind of threw us."

"Quinn O'Malley, the dark horse." I smiled. "Thanks for telling me."

"You're not upset, are you?"

"No. I'm not upset. I kind of like being underestimated." I glanced at the folder. "What is this?"

"The final plans for the Trenton project."

Jimmy took me through the design plans for the high-rise condos that O'Malley Properties were ready to build. I frowned as Jimmy continued to talk. I knew what I liked, and I knew what I didn't like. My love of Boston encompassed the historical aspect. I could get down with flashy and modern, but I really preferred that type of design reserved for clubs and bars.

"What do you think?" Jimmy asked.

I closed the folder. "Honestly? They look a little sterile."

"Sterile?"

"What's special about these?" I demanded. "Why are people going to spend one point two million on these condos?"

"Because they're luxury."

I shook my head. "It's not enough. These"—I placed my hand on the top of the red folder—"are beautiful. Don't get me wrong. The work is impeccable. The design is impeccable. But it's…cold."

"These are standard," Jimmy said. "These were designs your father always wanted, and they became standard for him."

My jaw tightened. "My father isn't here."

Jimmy held my gaze and then reached over for the folder. "They're not special."

"They're not special," I agreed with a nod. "And I think we can do better. Don't you?"

Jimmy's smile was slow. "I'm really glad I didn't enter that pool."

Chapter Thirty-Three

AFTER JIMMY LEFT, and no doubt went back to his own office to curse my name, I called Dimitri.

"I've been waiting," he said, his Russian accent caressing my ears. A stab of familiarity, of a life I'd once lived, rushed through me. Surprisingly, it didn't hurt.

"Quinn?" came Dimitri's voice. "Are you still there?"

"Yeah. I'm here." I cleared my throat. Cleared away the past. "I'm giving you *Krasnyy*."

"You can't give me *Krasnyy*."

"Sasha gave it to me. I'm giving it to you. For the cause."

"Cause? There's no cause."

"Let's call it a redistribution of assets." I got up from my office chair and walked over to close the door. Even though I no longer had an assistant, I still didn't want to take the chance that someone could walk by and overhear the conversation I was having with one of the most powerful men in the Russian mafia.

"I can't own *Krasnyy*. It doesn't belong to me. It belongs to you and his men. You were acting leader while Sasha was bedridden. The only reason the Russians were able to hold their territory was because you stepped in and ran things. You ran things when Sasha couldn't."

"Campbell helped, if you remember."

"I do." I pinched the bridge of my nose. "I'm trying to move on, Dimitri. Please take *Krasnyy*."

He was silent for so long, a part of me thought we'd been disconnected, but I knew he was still on the other end of the line. I knew he was debating what to do. He wanted to please me, but he also wanted to follow Sasha's last directives.

"Please," I whispered. "Please, Dimitri."

He sighed. "All right, Quinn."

Relief swept through me. I felt released from my past, from all the burdens that had been thrust onto my shoulders. Even though Dimitri couldn't see me, I smiled. I wanted to laugh and rejoice, and I wasn't sure why it took this moment for me to feel reborn, but I did.

"Thank you, Dimitri."

"Be well, Quinn."

We hung up and I closed my eyes. *Krasnyy* had been my last real tie to Sasha, and it was only right that I let it go. It was the only way I could move on—have a future, have a life.

My phone rang, and when I saw the name on the screen, I smiled.

"I've got good news," Ori said the moment I answered.

"Oh, yeah? What's that?"

"I just put my mom on a train bound for New York."

I laughed.

"It means we'll have some privacy."

My pulse kicked up.

"Quinn?"

"Can I take you to dinner?" I asked.

"You want to take me to dinner?"

"Yeah. We're celebrating."

"What are we celebrating?"

I looked out the large glass window. The sky was blue and bright. For now there was no hint of snow, no looming dark clouds.

"Life, Ori. We're celebrating life."

I took the rest of the afternoon off. When I got back to my father's house, Jessica wasn't there. The sitting room was covered in fabric swatches and paint samples. Furniture had been moved and some pieces were wrapped, waiting to be taken away to who knew where. The pieces that I'd stuck sticky notes on were left untouched, which I was grateful for.

I ran up the stairs to my bedroom to quickly pack a bag. As I grabbed enough clothes for a few days, I stopped to think about my long-term plan. I needed a place of my own. I'd never had a place of my own—decorated in my taste. I was suddenly excited for the prospect. I was ready for new endeavors.

Finally.

The world no longer seemed like a terrible and dark place. I'd rounded an emotional corner, and it felt like it had been a long time coming. My steps were no longer heavy. My spirit was no longer weighed down by memories I couldn't change. They'd become a part of me, but I no longer felt their crippling grip.

Grief was a strange beast. It held on, strangling you. Sometimes it won, but other times, it just…evaporated. Like morning mist. The feeling of it would linger, probably always. But it no longer hindered every feeling, every action, every moment.

I was glad I had choices. It felt like most of them had been taken away from me, but that hadn't been true. It was time to own what I could. My father's death, Sasha leaving, those weren't my fault.

They weren't my fault.

And I was tired of punishing myself, feeling like a martyr.

I picked up the bag and my keys and drove to Ori's house. He didn't even let me knock on the door before he was opening it and pulling me inside. Wrapping his arms around me, he buried his face in my shoulder.

"Uhm. Hello," I said. I dropped the bag and then put my arms around him.

"Hi." Leaning back, he smiled. "I didn't think you were going to come back."

"I told you I was going to. You didn't believe me?"

"You spook easy." He let me go and closed the door. "Do you hear that?"

"Hear what?"

He grinned. "Exactly."

I laughed. "You can't lie to me. You miss your mother. Admit it."

"I miss her. From a distance." He grasped my hand and brought it to his mouth. "You're cold. And you just got over being sick. You've got to take better care of yourself."

"Okay."

"I mean it," he warned, tugging me into his body again. He leaned down and placed his lips on mine. He kissed me like we'd been kissing each other for years. With confidence and assurance, with enjoyment and familiarity.

Ori Abruzzo knew how to kiss.

And I jumped into his arms and wrapped my legs

around his waist. He carried me into the living room and gently set me on the couch. He looked down at me with dark eyes, eyes that wanted me. He covered his body with mine. His weight was a comfort.

He set my nerves on fire. I was needy. So needy.

My hands wormed their way underneath his navy blue sweater, to feel the warm skin of his chest. Our mouths fused together, and we entwined our bodies, and I didn't care that he almost crushed me. But it felt good, breathing each other's air. After long, leisurely kisses, it wasn't enough.

I wanted to see him. And I wanted him to see me. All of me.

"Take me upstairs," I whispered against his lips.

He leaned back so he could look at me. "You sure?"

I nodded.

Ori stood, took my hand and pulled me up. His fingers sank into my hair and then moved down to cup the back of my neck. His hand was warm and I shivered. He gave me a long, deep kiss, and then he led me upstairs.

He took me into his bedroom, and before he could give me time to think, he gently urged me toward his four-poster, king-sized bed. My head hit the pillows, and I closed my eyes, reveling in the softness. But then I felt Ori come down on top of me, and my eyes flew open.

I dragged my fingers through his dark hair and then traced the contours of his face. There were things he needed to know—deserved to know. He'd have questions, the moment I took my clothes off. He'd see.

I was ready for him to see.

Gently, I pressed a hand to his chest and pushed him back. He watched as I slowly pulled off my sweater and then my slacks. His eyes devoured me and then his hands slid up my arms. I shivered from his touch on my bare skin. I reveled in it.

His fingers slipped my bra straps down my shoulders and then reached around to free the clasp. He tossed the black lace aside.

Ori didn't say anything. He didn't whisper compliments or words of endearment. Instead, he bathed my skin in kisses and skimmed his hands up and down my body, learning me. Learning us.

I helped him out of his clothes and then brought him back to me. I marveled at our differences. His darker skin to my fair. The sharp outlines of his muscles. He was wide where I was slender.

When he dragged his mouth across my flesh, I felt like a thousand firecrackers had been lit under my skin, just waiting to detonate. He was skilled and patient. Talented in a way that spoke of years of practice. But he worshiped me as if I'd been the only one, and there was no past between us. Even when he slid my underwear off me, finally unveiling what I'd been hiding all along, he didn't pause. He kept going and he didn't stop, not even when he put his mouth on me, and I was bucking beneath him with my release.

Still, it wasn't enough for him. Or for me. I wanted him inside of me, sheltered and deep.

He reached for a condom in the bedside drawer, and he rolled it down his firm length. And then he was sinking into me, slowly, like it was the most important thing in the world.

Ori took his time, letting me adjust, drawing my legs back so he could plunge deeper. I moaned and grasped his back. My nails tore the skin of his shoulders as he started to ride me. His slow pace suddenly became frantic, maniacal, like his only desire in the entire world was to make me come. He didn't find his own satisfaction until I shattered around him.

He pulled me to him as our breaths came in rapid pants, and he didn't move until I was nearly falling asleep. Ori gently kissed me before getting up to take care of himself, but he was back soon enough. He propped up on an elbow to look down at me, his free hand tracing the tiny white lines on my belly.

"You don't seem surprised," I said.

"I helped you when you got out of the bath. Remember?"

"Oh." I went silent.

"What happened?" he asked quietly.

"I fell," I said quietly.

"You were far enough along to show." It was a statement, not a question. When I looked at him in surprise, he made a move as if to shrug. "I have nieces and nephews."

"Ah."

"And the father? He's the one who left?"

"He didn't know," I said, for some reason wishing to defend Sasha, defend another man who'd once been in my bed. "He left and I found out after I came home to Boston."

"I'm so sorry, Quinn," he said, leaning over and brushing his lips against my bare shoulder.

"It was bad," I admitted, sorrow moving through me. "I was in bad shape. Mentally."

He pulled me toward him to tuck me into his side, rolling us over so he could spoon me. Ori put his face in the cradle of my body, and I continued to talk. It was almost like he knew it would be easier if I didn't have to look at him.

"And just when I was able to—I don't know—cope, my

dad got sick." I closed my eyes. "It's almost like life has to dish it all out at once, ya know?"

"Yeah. I know how that feels. Lost my dad. Then my brother. Lost a good friend. My best friend."

"How did it change you?" I asked. "I know how my losses changed me. I know that I shut down, put up walls, wouldn't let anyone in. How did your losses change you?"

He dropped a hand to my waist and urged me to roll over to face him. Our heads shared a pillow as we stared into each other's eyes. "I used to smile easily."

I traced the subtle smile lines around his mouth. "You smile."

As if on cue, his lips pulled back to reveal white, straight teeth. "You make me smile."

"Did you say that to all the women of your past? You know, the ones you needed for a night and then didn't call."

"You seem to have a very clear picture of the man I used to be."

"Well, were you that guy?"

He paused thoughtfully. "Yeah, I was that guy. Only the women I spent my time with never expected me to call."

"That's good, I suppose."

"It was just companionship, Quinn. So I didn't feel so alone. Some people—like you—retreat into themselves. Others—like me—seek out the most basic form of human companionship. I was grateful to them. They made me feel…I don't know, tethered."

"Vices. Crutches. Coping mechanisms. We're still standing, aren't we?"

He smiled, and this time it looked effortless and genuine. "Yeah, we are."

Chapter Thirty-Four

IN THE END, we decided not to go out. It was always like this in the beginning—deep conversations interspersed with the need to explore each other's bodies. It was some time in the middle of the night, the candles Ori had lit burning slow and bright, when we woke up from a nap and I was starving.

As I made a move to get out of bed, Ori pulled me back, and with a sultry laugh, I let him. We made love quickly, desperate, and nearly spent.

Panting, I rolled over onto my back. "I need real food now."

"Food and then a shower."

"Yes," I moaned. Both sounded perfect. I looked around for my clothes, hating the idea of having to put them on. Instead, Ori gave me his button-down shirt. I'd worn my fair share of men's shirts—I had no shame about my past—but this felt different. Like the start of something new. Like the start of something that could last.

Quinn O'Malley 3.0 was strangely hopeful and optimistic.

"What do you want to eat?" Ori asked, opening the fridge. He'd thrown on a pair of sweats, but had left his chest bare.

"I don't know. Something that doesn't need assembling."

"Ah, got it." He reached in and started pulling out cheeses and fruit. "I've got a bottle of red open if you want to pour us two glasses."

I moved around his kitchen, enjoying the space and the layout. It was roomy without being opulent. Unlike the house I'd grown up in.

Ori sliced oranges and strawberries and arranged them on a platter. Four types of cheeses followed. I sipped from my wine glass as I watched him.

"What happened?" I asked.

"Hmm?"

"To your best friend."

He paused ever so slightly but didn't take his focus away from the cutting board. "He was set up by a trusted friend. Murdered in cold blood."

My breath hitched, but I said nothing.

The knife hitting wood echoed through the quiet kitchen.

"I shouldn't have asked," I said, my heart breaking for him.

He gently set the knife down and looked at me. "You should always ask. Always."

"So I didn't overstep?" I peeked at him from beneath my eyelashes, worried that I'd changed the tone of our entire night.

"No, you didn't overstep. It was a long time ago, Quinn. Not as recent as some of your losses. You shared with me; I'm glad to share with you." He went back to slicing cheese and then he smiled.

"What? What's that smile about?" I demanded. "That smile means something." That smile sent a wave of relief through me.

"That smile is pure amusement. You get what we're doing, don't you?"

"Dating? Having sex?"

"Yes, to both of those. But don't you think—I'm going to freak you the fuck out but that's a risk I'm willing to take. Don't you think there's something here? Something real?"

He stared at me, brown eyes intense. My gaze dropped to the column of his neck. But in the spirit of wanting to embrace the new me, the me that could have a future, I nodded. "Yeah, Ori. I think there's something real here."

Ori smiled again and went back to slicing. When he had everything arranged on the platter, he grabbed it and his glass of wine. "Get yours and the bottle."

I thought we were headed to the living room, but he surprised me when he moved toward the stairs. He set the platter down in the middle of the rumpled bed and placed his glass of wine on the bedside table.

"This was a great idea," I said, sitting on the bed and curling my legs underneath myself.

"Crumbs in the bed don't bother you?" he asked.

"I don't know if I've ever gotten crumbs in the bed. Or if I have, someone changed the sheets immediately. And before you say anything, yes I know I'm spoiled."

"Spoiled is okay. Entitled. Well, that's another thing entirely. How is it, running your father's business?"

"Speaking of entitled?" I teased. I grasped the glass of wine and took a hefty sip. It was a beautiful wine. Light, flavorful. "I think I'm going to be really good at it. It's hard, you know? Challenging. I never thought I'd want to do it, but I do."

"It's amazing, isn't it? When you feel like you've found your purpose, your place?"

"What's your purpose?"

He plopped a strawberry slice into his mouth and chewed, looking thoughtful. "I think I'd like to go through with the restaurant idea. I want to own my own restaurant."

"Even if I don't launder money for you?"

Ori laughed. "You ask that so cavalierly. Without any judgment."

"No judgment. Just curiosity."

"Yeah, my own restaurant even if you don't want to launder money."

Here we were, two people who lived outside the normal bounds of the law.

"Quinn? I'd still like us to find a way to enter some sort of partnership."

"What kind of partnership?" I asked with a tremulous smile.

"Whatever kind you want. Now eat some cheese so we can shower."

"Don't go into work," Ori said, his hands drifting lower. Because of those wandering hands, I'd hardly slept. And yet I couldn't feel too bad about the exhaustion. When I stretched, my body ached. It was the best kind of ache, reminding me that I was a desirable woman.

"I have to go into work," I said. "There are deadlines —and I made an architect redesign an entire concept."

"Hard ass," he murmured, his teeth nipping the curve of my breast.

"Ori," I moaned as his fingers delved between my legs.

"I want you again," he said. His lips closed over a nipple and he sucked.

Sparks shot from my breast to my core. I opened my legs wider, and he slid in a second finger.

"I could do this all day, every day." His mouth moved to my other breast.

I agreed with him and would've voiced it aloud, but I was too caught up with the idea of coming.

He slipped his fingers out of me and rolled on a condom. I clasped his back and ceased to think about work at all. I winced as he penetrated deep.

"You okay?" he whispered.

I nodded and leaned up to kiss him. We were slick with sweat and desire as he pushed hard, setting a relentless pace. Just as I was about to come, he flipped us over so I was on top. His hands clasped my hips as he urged me to ride him. I leaned over and kissed him, our tongues fighting for dominance.

I wanted him harder and deeper. I took everything he had to give and threw it back. There was a moment when it all stopped, and then I catapulted over the cliff. I broke apart, screaming his name.

He grasped my hips, hard enough to bruise, and then he was spearing up into me, his own release driving him to a crazed frenzy.

I collapsed on top of him and curled my hands against his chest. I inhaled the smell of us on his skin. A prickle of emotion bubbled up inside of me. I closed my eyes and tried to breathe through it.

"Quinn?" he asked gruffly, his fingers tangling through my hair.

"Yeah, I'm okay."

"Quinn."

"Yeah."

"Sit up."

"No," I mumbled against his chest.

"Please?"

After a moment of reluctance, I sat up and looked at him. His hands cleared away the tears from my cheeks. "What's wrong?"

"Nothing actually. Nothing's wrong. Sometimes I do this."

"Do what?"

"Feel things. After."

"Intense things?"

I nodded.

"Anything you can put into words?"

I shook my head.

"All right." He took my arms and gently pulled me back down on his chest.

"I have to go to work"

"In a minute. You need to be held first."

Smiling against his skin, I buried my nose against him and let out a chuckle.

"What?" His hands grazed my back in a gesture of comfort. He was good at the comforting thing. Maybe too good.

"I guess I don't do taking it slow very well."

"We are taking it slow. Just because we slept together doesn't mean I'm ready to give you a ring."

"Good to know." I brushed a kiss across his chest, and then I slowly eased off of him. "I need to go to work. I want to go to work." What I really needed to do was get away from Ori so I could think clearly. It all became muddled when we were in bed, a tangle of arms and legs. I wasn't ready for anything more than what we had. I wasn't ready to love someone as deeply as I'd loved Sasha.

I didn't know if I was even capable.

"I fired my assistant," I told him as I went to my bag. I pulled out a pair of clean clothes, only to realize none of them were work appropriate. Guess it was going to be a casual Wednesday.

"You fired your assistant?" He strode past me into the bathroom. A moment later, I heard the sound of running water. I went into the bathroom and watched him climb into the shower.

"She was my father's assistant," I said. "And she didn't like me."

"So you fired her."

"I offered her a nice severance package."

He chuckled. "Are you just gonna stand out there, or are you getting in?" I stepped into the shower, and Ori moved out of the way so I could have a quick wash. "Did she take the package?"

"She stormed out of the office, and I had to tell security she wasn't allowed back in the building."

"You worried about her?" he asked, suddenly sober, eyes dark as they rested on me.

"Hardly. She's a middle-aged woman more prone to enjoying a baked good than wielding a weapon. I had her banned from the building more as a sign of my power."

"Your absolute power," he teased. "Queen of the O'Malley Empire."

"Oh, shut up," I said with a laugh.

We moved around each other to switch places, mindful of the slippery tub. I wasn't quite ready to get out, choosing to stare at Ori's wet, naked body. Watching the water droplets dribble down his chest to his flat stomach.

"Hey. Eyes up here," he teased. "I respect your commitment to your job, but how about lunch? Can we do lunch?"

I sighed. "I really need to use the time to look for an apartment."

"That's what a realtor is for," he reminded me.

"I know. I'm going to call on my way to work, and then hopefully she can show me a few places during the lunch hour."

"Any idea what you're looking for?"

I got out of the shower and reached for a towel. "I don't know. Something cozy, I think." I was tired of sprawling spaces for one. "Two bedroom. I'm taking my father's desk, the crystal decanter set, and my bedroom furniture. Everything else is staying."

The water shut off. "You're not sentimental at all, are you?"

"What does sentiment ever get you?" I wrapped the towel around me and then reached for the comb on the sink counter.

"I happen to agree with you," he said. "I just thought it was interesting." He opened the bathroom door to let out the steam.

"Do you have a hair dryer?" I asked, starting to open and close drawers.

"Nope."

"I can't go out with a wet head."

"You can borrow one of my hats," Ori said as I came into the bedroom. He was already in a pair of boxer briefs. Clothes felt like shields, armor for the world.

"Hat hair. Awesome. And I forgot my makeup," I stated. "I've never forgotten my makeup."

"You're beautiful without it," Ori said. He slid his belt into his pant loops and buckled it. "You don't need all that stuff on your face anyway."

"You're such a guy," I said. "Mascara and lip gloss are necessities." I pulled on my jeans and a cream sweater and then towel dried my hair as best I could. I glanced at the alarm clock. "Crap. I'm gonna be late."

"One cup of coffee," Ori begged. "And a bagel."

"How did this turn into breakfast?" I demanded.

"I'm an Italian," he explained with a rueful smile. "No one leaves my house on an empty stomach."

Chapter Thirty-Five

"Well, what do you think?" I asked, gesturing to the currently empty living room.

Shannon looked around, her brow furrowed. "It's…nice."

"Small. You can say small," I said.

She nodded. "Very small. Very…not you."

"I'm trying something different."

"I don't understand," she said as she walked through the miniscule living room into the connected kitchen that was barely a kitchen. If Ori ever wanted to cook me dinner again, we couldn't do it here. The thought of his big body in my tiny kitchen made me smile.

"I grew up in a large house, Shannon. And then I lived in that loft with Sasha. This feels like…me. Like the me I would've gotten to know if I'd had to earn it on my own."

"What's happened to you?" she demanded with a wry smile. "I don't see you for days because you're totally up to your eyeballs in your dad's company, then there's a new guy, and now there's this new apartment."

"Speaking of the new guy," I said. "Do you and Patrick want to meet him?"

"Do I? You've been keeping him hidden. Or he's been keeping you hidden."

"Ah, yeah, we've been busy."

"You're blushing."

"I like him."

"Yes, I can see that. Let me see the rest of this place really fast, and then we're going for coffee where you can tell me about him. Because let's face it, that's the most interesting part of this conversation."

I laughed and waved her toward the bedroom. It was larger than I'd expected it to be, and it had a decent closet. Not nearly enough closet space for all my clothes, so I'd have to get an armoire. I wasn't moving without all my clothes.

"How's Jessica taking your departure?" Shannon asked as I locked up the apartment. We took the stairs slow—and I walked in front of Shannon, so that if she fell, I'd break her fall. I'd protect her any way I could from suffering the same kind of loss I'd endured.

"I haven't seen much of her since she got back," I admitted. "She's been in full-on decorating mode or lunching and throwing herself back into her charities. Plus, I've been staying at Ori's."

"Have you now?" she teased.

"Oh, hush."

We made our way down the street, and I hit the clicker. Shannon opened the passenger side and climbed in, and when I got into the driver's side, Shannon said, "You're also driving yourself. When was the last time you did that?"

I threw her a smile as I started the car. "Let's get it all out there, okay? I was spoiled rotten growing up. And I let my dad take care of me. I let Sasha take care of me. I didn't fight them, ya know?" I looked in the rearview mirror and then pulled away from the curb. "I've let men take care of me my entire life when I was fully capable of taking care of myself."

"So that's what the small apartment and driving your-self is about? Taking care of yourself? You're still wearing three hundred dollar jeans," she pointed out with a laugh.

"Well, there's no saying I have to rough it, okay?" I laughed with her. "My dad gave me his business, but I'm making it mine."

"How?" She turned in her seat to look at me.

"Dad's projects are mostly condos, townhouses, shop-ping malls. They are," I said with a shrug, "ugly. Necessary, I guess. But ugly. I want—I don't know—beauty? I'm not a designer or an architect, but I've got this chance to add to the community, ya know? Like add beauty. We live in a city. A beautiful, historic city, and I'd just like to find a way to help preserve that."

"Quinn O'Malley, you surprise me."

"Sometimes I surprise myself." I turned left. "Do you remember the night of my mother's funeral?"

She frowned. "That's out of left field."

"But do you remember it?"

"Sort of."

"I think about that night. A lot," I admitted. "I often wonder how I would've turned out if Mom had lived. Would I still have been a wild child? Would I still have decided to push all my boundaries?"

Drinking. Smoking. Sex. All far too young. I'd been lucky. Dad had snapped me out of it. But something happened when privileged kids didn't have to work for anything. Money opened doors. Sometimes the wrong ones.

"I think so," Shannon said slowly. "You were kinda reckless—even when your mom was alive."

I'd been the kind of kid who'd throw on a pair of roller skates and go down the big hills. I'd crash, but I'd always get up again. Maybe that was the theme of my life. I'd been knocked down more times than I could count, yet I always managed to get up again.

"You worried a lot for me, didn't you?" I asked, with a look in her direction as I pulled the car into a spot in front of a coffee shop.

"You can't tell, but there's a good amount of gray mixed in with the blonde," she teased.

"I just gave you practice." I looked at her belly. She wasn't even showing. Shannon was tiny, though, and I had a feeling she'd be all stomach.

"Let's pray my child is a little less…"

"Quinn-like?"

"I was going to say foolhardy. I sometimes think…" She shook her head and released her seat belt.

"What?"

"I sometimes wonder if that's kind of how you fall in love, too. You're kind of reckless, ya know? You're all in and you love with your entire heart."

"Yeah." I let out a shallow laugh. "Sometimes I wish my heart was a little more discerning."

"The heart doesn't work like that. Brains do." She got out of the car, and even though we were only going a few feet, she pulled the collar of her coat closed.

"Well, you got it right, first try out of the gate," I said.

"Yeah. But we weren't without our own issues." She raised her eyebrows as if daring me to remember the rocky time she'd had with Patrick. When he'd blown out his knee, it had ended his career with The Patriots. Lost, unhappy, in pain, he'd gotten addicted to pain pills. "Made us stronger, though. So I am grateful for that."

I held the door open for her, and she walked inside. Shannon was shorter than me by a few good inches. She only came to my chin. And she was slight, reminding me of a wren or a finch. Yet she'd always been the one to look out for me, following along, even riding into danger because she didn't want me to go through anything alone. She always tried to talk me out of things, but I never listened.

"What do you want?" I asked her, stepping up to the counter.

"Pumpkin spice latte and a muffin—I'll grab that table in the corner."

Once I had our order, I brought it over to the table. There were a few other customers, some sitting with journals or laptops. All of them were wearing ear buds. I often wondered why people went to coffee shops to work. How did they get anything done with all the distractions and people-watching capabilities?

"Okay, now tell me everything there is to know about Ori." Shannon unwrapped the lemon poppyseed muffin and took a bite.

I wrapped my hands around my mug, thinking before speaking. "He was a jerk when we first met," I said and then recounted our meeting at the mayor's gala.

"But like a fungus, he grew on you?" Shannon took a sip of her coffee and sighed. "This place makes the best coffee."

"He totally grew on me." I leaned in close and whispered, "He was supposed to go into business with my dad."

Shannon's eyes widened, and then she nodded in understanding. I'd never given her a full rundown of the family business, but she knew better than to ask for an in-depth explanation of how the O'Malleys made their money.

"Are you going to—"

The shake of my head cut her off. "No. I don't think it's a good idea to mix business and pleasure."

"Your father and Sasha were in business together," she pointed out.

"Their business was between them—and Flynn Campbell. It's complicated."

Sasha had met my father first. My entire relationship with Sasha had been orchestrated. Manufactured. When I'd found out, I'd been livid. There might have been some breaking of dishes. I'd thought about walking away, but Sasha hadn't let me.

He'd said you don't walk away from the kind of love that shakes you to your soul. Orchestrated or not.

Strange. He'd managed to get me to stay, but I couldn't keep him from walking away.

"So Ori…he's like your father? Like Sasha?"

I knew what she was asking without asking it. Was he a criminal, she wanted to know. I nodded. "Yeah. He is."

"Are you sure you want to get involved with him? I mean, don't you want someone not a part of that life?"

"Ideally? Sure. But what am I gonna do? I'm an O'Malley. I can't just date someone normal. Like an accountant."

I was raised in a different world than Shannon. She didn't grow up with criminals for uncles. She didn't grow up with thick-accented Irishmen who spoke in code.

"You like him?" Shannon asked. "Like really like him?"

I nodded.

"Then I'll like him."

"You sure? Because—"

"I'll love him," she said fiercely. "And if he breaks your

heart, I'll punch him in the jaw like your brother taught me."

Throwing back my head, I shouted with laughter. Tiny, pugnacious Shannon would serve as my protector. I couldn't ask for a better friend.

Chapter Thirty-Six

"You look exhausted," Ori said when he opened the door.

I stood on his porch steps and didn't move. Despite the snow coming down, despite the fact that my toes were cold, I was unable to make my body work. I blinked bleary eyes at him.

"Quinn?"

"I thought I was moving. Am I not moving?"

With a sigh, Ori grasped my arm and gently urged me inside. "What happened to you today?" He closed the door and reached for my coat.

Sighing, I somehow shrugged out of it. "I ran around the city looking at possible sites to develop. I went over legal jargon with the company lawyer, I approved designs, I met with potential assistants. What didn't I do today?"

"Glass of wine?" he asked with a quirk of his mouth.

"Like you even have to ask."

As he hung my coat on the rack, he said, "Take a seat in the living room. Fire's going."

I kicked off my heels, my cold feet touching the bare

wood floor. "I'm not moving from this couch for at least thirty minutes," I called to Ori once I was sitting on a plush cushion.

Ori came into the room, carrying a glass of wine. He handed it to me and then sank down next to me. "You don't have to move at all. Hello."

I grinned. "Hello."

He leaned over to kiss me, and I melted into his body. After we kissed, I snuggled against him. "This is nice."

"I agree." He inched away. "I need to go take care of something. I'll be back in fifteen, okay?"

"Okay. I'm just gonna sit here and not move. Ever again."

Chuckling, he pressed a kiss to my forehead and then got up. I yawned and leaned back against the couch. How the hell did my father work such long hours? This morning, I'd gotten to the office at just past eight. It was now seven in the evening. I'd barely managed to scarf down a sandwich for lunch and then I was back at it. In heels, no less. Running around the city in heels? Not for the faint of heart. I'd felt one step behind the entire day.

Maybe my brain didn't work the same way as my father's. Maybe he'd been exhilarated, loving all the challenges. Maybe I wasn't cut out for this, after all. Would it be the coward's way out to hire someone, a manager to oversee everything while I tried my hand at event planning? I'd be good at event planning. I had expensive taste and I was fairly organized.

"Hey," Ori said, startling me.

I looked behind me. "Jeez. You walk silently."

"Sorry."

"Finish what you needed to?"

He nodded. "Can I show you?"

I groaned. "I thought I didn't have to move."

"Come on, let me show you," he urged.

I somehow managed to get up. Ori took my hand and led me up the stairs and into the bedroom. "In there," he gestured to the bathroom.

"Okay," I said in confusion. I pushed open the bathroom door and stopped. Ori had dimmed the lights, lit a bunch of candles, and drawn me a bubble bath.

"Oh, wow," I breathed.

Ori took the glass of wine from my hand and set it down on the bathroom sink. "Strip," he commanded.

I gave him a saucy look. "I need help."

Grinning wickedly, Ori reached for the buttons of my shirt. He undid them slowly and then pushed it off my shoulders. I shrugged out of it and let it drop to the floor. Next he went for the button of my gray slacks.

"I like you in white lace," he said, voice tight. His fingers grazed the straps of my demi-cup bra and slipped inside to stroke my skin.

I moaned and leaned into his touch.

One hand grasped my hip while the other slid down into my panties. He stroked the seam of my body causing me to shiver and grip him tighter.

"You like that?" he whispered in my ear, easing a finger inside of me.

"Jesus," I muttered. My nails dug into his shoulders, and my eyes fluttered closed. "You're so good at that."

"What about this?" he demanded as he added a finger. His thumb brushed the bundle of nerves waiting for his touch. I shuddered as desire pumped through my veins.

"Quinn," he growled. "Open your eyes. Let me see you."

My eyes flipped open, and I stared into his dark brown orbs as I came. He grinned, arrogant, sure, a man who knew how to please a woman.

His fingers eased out of me, and in a complete show of possession, he stuck them in his mouth to taste me. Watching his eyes darken even more made me quiver. "Get in your bath, Quinn. We're not done." He let go of me and then gave me a little pat before leaving.

Once I got my bearings, I stripped out of the rest of my clothes and sank into the bathwater. I covered myself in scented bubbles and leaned against the back of the tub. Unfortunately my wine was still on the bathroom sink. I was debating whether or not to retrieve it when the bathroom door opened again.

"I thought you were going to let me enjoy my bath in peace," I said, taking in his magnificent body. Completely nude. All golden skin, jutted hips, chiseled muscles. His erection jutted out; he grasped it and gave it a pump.

"I thought about you in the bath," he rasped. "And then I thought about why I wasn't in there with you."

I leaned up and scooted forward. Ori walked over and climbed into the tub to sit behind me. His hands stroked my skin, rubbing the knots in my back. Then his mouth worked its way across my shoulder blades to my neck. Ori brushed aside my bobbed hair and teased the sensitive skin with his lips.

"I was exhausted when I got here," I reminded him, feeling the familiar heat settle between my legs. "How is it that I all I want to do is—"

His fingers came around to pinch my nipple. I bowed against him, loving that he played my body, knowing exactly what would make me shake. Maybe I was making up for lost time or maybe I just enjoyed Ori's attention. Either way, I wasn't going to deprive myself.

Ori's large hands cupped my breasts before sliding down my torso. I spread my legs, giving him access. I was slick from bubbles and my desire, but suddenly, I didn't want his finger—I wanted more.

"Ori," I groaned.

His hand settled over my mound, and I ground myself against his palm, enjoying the sparks singeing my nerve endings.

"Let's get out," I demanded. Somehow I found the ability to stand. Water sluiced off me as I reached for a towel. I stepped out of the tub and quickly dried myself off as I headed for the bedroom. Looking over my shoulder, I found Ori striding toward me, a towel around his waist.

"How do you want it, Quinn?" he asked, voice rough.

"From behind," I told him, my voice heavy with need. "And I don't want to wait."

I wanted to be dominated; I wanted to feel his power as he slipped into me. I wanted to feel every inch of him, long, hard, pulsing.

I climbed onto the bed and spread my legs. He put his mouth on me, his tongue delving, stroking. My hands gripped the covers. And then he replaced his mouth with the part of him I desired, and I ceased to think at all.

Chapter Thirty-Seven

"YOU DO REALIZE we have yet to go out on an actual date," Ori said, sometime later.

I was drowsy and comfortable, wrapped in Ori's arms. "We always seem to get distracted. Besides, it's cold out there, and it's warm in here."

"I would like to take you out on a real date, though. Just so you know I'm not a slacker boyfriend."

"Boyfriend?"

"What? Not a fan of the title?"

"No, I just—didn't think about it."

"You mean you didn't think about what we are."

"It's too soon to put a label on this, Ori."

"Is it? You met my mother. I've taken care of you while you were sick. You've slept at my place the last four nights."

"Four nights is hardly a routine," I pointed out.

He laughed. "You're such a guy."

"Me? I'm the guy? Because I'm not ready to label this?"

"Fine. We don't have to put a label on our relationship," Ori said. "But it doesn't change the fact that we are in a relationship. And this is headed…."

"Where *is* this headed?" I demanded.

"What do you want, Quinn? Out of a relationship, I mean?"

I frowned in thought. What did I want? Stability, for one. Fidelity and loyalty, for another. Love, of course, but wasn't that supposed to be a given? Was I still so naïve even after Sasha?

"Not going to answer?" Ori pressed.

"I'm not sure I have an answer."

"You do, you just don't want to say it."

I sat up and moved out of his arms, away from his warmth. "Fidelity, okay? I want fidelity."

He didn't say anything for a long moment. "That's not the norm. For people like us."

"My father was faithful to my mother. Sasha was faithful to me."

"How do you know?" he inquired, cocking his head. "Their word? People lie."

"You asked what I wanted, and I told you," I snapped.

Ori sighed. "I'm an Abruzzo."

"Is that supposed to mean something to me?"

"My family is a powerful one. One of the oldest families in Italy."

"Are you telling me you can't promise me fidelity? Or you won't?"

"I'm saying fidelity isn't a model I'd ever thought I would have to live by."

"So this entire time we've been seeing each other, you've been with other women?"

"Well, no," he admitted. "But I could've been."

"Why didn't you?"

"Because I didn't—and don't—want anyone else."

"Then what are we even talking about?" I asked in exasperation.

"I'm saying the men in my circle don't promise fidelity, and the women don't expect it."

"I see," I said quietly. "So that's my option? Stay with you, knowing you won't keep it in your pants? Knowing I'm supposed to promise fidelity, yet you won't promise me the same?"

"I never said I wouldn't promise it," Ori interjected. "I was only explaining to you how it is in my family. I'll be expected to…"

"Not all men cheat. Not all men want to cheat."

"Sasha again, huh? That's what this comes back to?"

"He didn't cheat." My voice was firm with assurance.

"How do you know?" he taunted. "You trusted him to tell you the truth? You thought he wasn't the type of man who'd ever leave you. Well, guess what, he did."

It was like he'd gripped my throat and started squeezing. "How dare you," I whispered. I unfolded my body and got off the bed. I looked around for my clothes, realizing they were still in the bathroom.

"Quinn," Ori said and was somehow in front of me. His hand went to my arm. "Quinn, I—"

"Take your fucking hand off me."

He hesitated just for a moment, and then he removed his fingers from my skin.

I drew myself up and pushed out my chest. Like a man, his gaze dropped. I turned and went into the bathroom. I didn't bother with a door slam. Door slams were for women who were trying to prove a point. Mine had already been proven.

I quickly got into my clothes, wanting to shield myself from him, wanting distance. Most of all, I wanted time to think about what the hell I was doing.

"Quinn," Ori begged, following me out of the bedroom and down the stairs. "Please. Don't go. Not like this."

"You say really horrible things when you're angry, Ori. Hurtful things." I whirled on him. "I told you things—" I swallowed. "I was just feeling like I could trust you, that I wanted to trust you. And at the first sign of not getting your way, you were mean. You were exactly the guy I met at the mayor's gala." I shook my head. "Should've gone with my gut."

"Don't say that," Ori said. "You're not wrong for giving me a chance. What does this say about you, Quinn? Huh? You think everyone is perfect? You think everyone is always going to tell you what you want to hear? I'm human. I made a mistake. You're going to walk away because of that?"

"Because of that? No." I shook my head. "I'm walking away because you can't tell me yes or no that you plan on being faithful to me. Call me stupid, call me naïve, call me whatever you want, but I know it'll eat away at me. When you're out and I'm not with you, I'll think the worst. I'll expect the worst."

"Punishing me because of him," he said, tone hard. "You'll always punish me for what he did."

I couldn't think clearly. Not after sex, not after wine, not after lying in his arms and letting him hold me. He'd stroked my body. He'd traced the scars on my belly. But that wouldn't be enough.

"You may have told me about your past," Ori said, standing as still as a granite statue. "But that doesn't mean you let me in."

"I might not be capable. Did you ever think of that?"

"Then how can you ask me to be faithful when you can't promise the same. Fidelity isn't just about the physical, Quinn. But I think you know that. How did we get here? We were having the perfect night and then—" He shook his head. "How did it become complete and utter shit?"

"That's the way of things," I said quietly. "One way or another."

"You want to leave? Go ahead. But if you do, don't come back."

I smiled slowly, showing my teeth. "Ultimatum? Really?"

We stared at each other, adversaries when moments ago we'd been lovers.

And like a coward, I grabbed my purse and walked out of Ori's house, out of his life.

Chapter Thirty-Eight

QUINN O'MALLEY, you stupid fucking coward.

I'd like that on my tombstone, please.

He'd backed me into a corner. Or maybe I'd put myself there. Either way, the only way out had been to set fire to everything and watch it burn.

I was self-destructive and self-sabotaging.

Ori and I were no longer...whatever we were.

We hadn't been together. Not really. We'd be on the verge, but of course I'd been the one to pick a fight, proclaim he couldn't be faithful when all along I was worried about myself. Not physically. I'd never crossed a line while with someone.

But it was true what Ori accused without actually accusing.

I was still in love with Sasha.

No matter that I'd found Ori fascinating and sweet. Smart and challenging. I wondered if he was trying too hard, trying too hard to prove his worth to me.

I'd given him a chance. After the mayor's gala, he didn't deserve it. Not the way he'd spoken to me, and yet,

I'd been intrigued, especially when he'd begun to show a different side of himself.

And when he'd taken care of me when I'd been sick…

A pang shot through my chest. If I couldn't fall in love with Ori, then what hope did I have?

Had I been on my way to falling in love with him?

If I had to ask myself that question, then the answer was probably no.

The words Shannon said earlier this week came back to haunt me, about hearts not being discerning. Had I let my head be too involved? Had I just been looking for an excuse to shut Ori out? To walk away?

"Fuck," I muttered.

O'Malleys had pride issues. We never backed down, even if we were wrong.

I needed to turn around. It was dark and the roads were icy, and I was in a neighborhood I didn't recognize. My phone rang. I didn't reach for it, knowing it was Ori and that I had to focus. The street wasn't well lit, and the temperature had dropped to below freezing.

Black ice.

I'd learned how to drive on black ice.

It started to snow. White, thick, fat flakes disappeared the moment they hit the ground. I turned on my windshield wipers. My phone kept ringing. As soon as it went to voicemail, it would pause, and then start up again.

I came to a stretch of straight road with glowing street lamps. I made sure no one was behind me and then slowed down. I reached over into the passenger seat where my purse rested and dug around for my phone. With my eyes on the road, I turned it on silent and tossed it back into the seat.

The snow fall increased, the sky grew darker, and the

roads got worse. I turned on the radio and fiddled until I found a weather report.

"Boston can expect two to four feet of snow. It's already started to come down and will pick up around midnight. The temperature is going to keep dropping. If you don't have to be out, don't. Stay inside. Stay safe." The DJ's voice was oddly peppy. Then again, the amount of caffeine they had to down to be alert was nauseating.

I turned off the radio just as an annoying teen pop star came on. My thumbs tapped the wheel in thought. I needed to go home. Home to my new apartment that currently only had furniture and clothes in it. No personal touches, no Irish wool blankets to snuggle into, no mugs, no tea bags. I'd done absolutely nothing with the space yet because I'd been working or sleeping at Ori's.

Ori.

I sighed and pulled over. I went for my phone again, completely dismissing all the missed calls and voicemails. I opened my GPS app and synced it to Bluetooth. Normally, I wouldn't need a map to get me home, but it was dark and snowing. Every little bit helped.

I got back on the road and took it even slower. The lights of the street lamps bounced off the white snow, causing partial road blindness. The speaker spit out my next direction as my phone rang again.

Ignoring it was a safer bet, but he'd been calling nonstop for thirty minutes. I needed to put him out of his misery. I pressed a button.

"Quinn? Quinn are you there?" came Ori's worried voice.

"Yeah, I'm here. Trying to drive without distractions."

"Well, if you'd answered the phone the first time I called—"

"I can't do this right now. It's snowing, it's hard to see, and I need to pay attention."

"Come back. Please come back. I said things…but I never wanted to push you away."

"I know. Just—this is hard for me, okay? Can you give me some time? Please? I—I know I was wrong, but I can't…not right now."

He sighed, as if knowing he wasn't going to barrel over me or wear me down. "All right, Quinn, please just be safe—"

My headlights flashed on a pair of black eyes. The buck stood in the middle of the road with no intention of moving. I swerved, but the tires slid instead of gripped. As I spun out of control, the buck jumped the exact wrong angle and hit the driver's side. The car continued to spin. It was murky, and I couldn't get my bearings. I heard the scrape of metal, and then the front end of the car nose-dived and whirled.

My head hit the steering wheel, and then everything went black.

Chapter Thirty-Nine

RED PULSED BEHIND MY EYES. With each beat, my head throbbed. I cracked my lids, peering through slits. It was dark. Except for the red. So much red.

Why was the red flashing?

I heard the crunch of metal, and then a blast of cold air. Hands skated over my body. Voices. Sounds. Shrill. Sirens.

Something went around my neck, and then I was being shifted. Moved, strapped, rolled toward the waiting ambulance. An EMT peered over me, shined a light in my eyes, asked me questions.

My lids closed and the darkness took me again.

When I awoke, I heard beeping machines, saw bright florescent lights, and I couldn't feel my body. My eyes slowly tracked a doctor in a white lab coat looking at my chart. He glanced up and smiled.

"You're awake." He stepped to the side of the bed and shined a light into my pupils. "Good. That's good. Do you know where you are?"

"Hospital," I rasped.

He nodded. "Yes. You were in a car accident. Do you remember?"

"Yes. I hit…a deer."

"The EMTs found your car in a ditch. I'm guessing you swerved, lost control on the ice…your head hit the steering wheel. You've got a concussion, nothing is broken. You're very lucky." He smiled again, glass lenses gleaming. He gently put his hand to my shoulder. "Get some rest, okay? I'll see you in the morning."

He headed for the door. With his hand on the knob, he said, "Ah, someone is here to see you. Normally I'd tell him to come back during visiting hours, but he's very insistent. Is it okay if I send him in?"

"Okay." My throat was sore like I'd been screaming, but I didn't remember screaming when my car skidded off the side of the road. I was replaying my accident when the door opened.

He was handsome with dark brown hair, dark eyes shining with emotion. "Quinn," he said, coming to my bed. He crouched down next to me, his hand snaking out to grasp mine. "God, you scared me. I'm so glad you're okay."

I looked at him, trying to place him, but there was only a darkness in my memory where this man should've been.

My heart thumped loudly in my ears, and I wet my suddenly dry lips. "Who…who are you?"

The handsome man's face fell, and his hand tightened on mine. "You don't remember who I am?"

I shook my head ever so slightly.

"Quinn," he began. "I'm Ori. Your fiancé."

About the Author

Emma Slate is writing on the run. The dangerous alpha men she writes about aren't thrilled that she's sharing their stories for your enjoyment. So far, she's been able to evade them by jet setting around the world. She wears only black leather because it's bad ass…and hides blood.

Stalk her here:
www.emmaslate.com/
emma@emmaslate.com

Made in the USA
Columbia, SC
18 July 2018